Morning Crafts

Tito Perdue

Morning Crafts

ARKTOS

London, 2012

First edition published in 2012
by Arktos Media Ltd., London, United Kingdom.

Printed in the United Kingdom

ISBN 978-1-907166-57-0

BIC classification:
Modern and contemporary fiction (FA)
Philosophy and theory of education (JNA)

Editor: John B. Morgan
Cover Illustration: Alex Kurtagic
Cover Design: Andreas Nilsson
Layout: Daniel Friberg

ARKTOS MEDIA LTD

www.arktos.com

Table of Contents

This book is for Alex Kurtagic.

One

An old misconception — that he had been "snatched up," they said, and "beguiled" into places where he didn't want to go. "Abducted," they go on, and carried away at age thirteen in pathetic circumstances while still clutching his fishing rod and cup of dead crickets.

Remember, too, that in those days he used to venture only so far into the woods before his nerves ran out. Seldom was he more than a minute from his father's property and a brief run back to the valley with its civilization and farms. But because on this day he had happened upon a pond that promised good fishing…

Here Lee settled, highly conscious of the smell of mimosa and honeysuckle, and of the tall man in suit and tie who appeared to be hiding in the kudzu. Instead, taking a cigarette, he lit the thing with aplomb and then tossed the match in among the several dozen whirligigs skating about insanely on narrow feet that left momentary grooves upon the surface of the water. He had focused in upon perhaps the most energetic of those insects when he began to believe that he could detect a pair of matched breams paying notice to his bait. Two crows flew over, both of them coming to a stop when they perceived young Lee on shore. Meanwhile, he had to contend with the smoke from his cigarette and the half-dozen gnats mustering in his face.

He was to catch two breams on that day, one of them weighing the best part of a pound and the other the worst. Pleased by it, he had begun to load his hook with more than just one cricket at a time, an extravagance he thought that he could justify. It was true that he had a headache, the penalty for his cigarettes. Suddenly he yanked back on the line, very nearly catching a bream or possibly a catfish that would have dwarfed both his two previous fish put together. He cursed, spat, smote himself on the temple and then, using one hand only, ignited another cigarette. That was when the man came out of hiding.

Lee hated to see these things in what he considered his own private woods. He especially hated a smiling city man in a grey suit with a primrose in his lapel and two books under his arm. Ignoring him, Lee hummed as he loaded his hook and then lowered the bait gingerly to a somewhat deeper level than he had so far tried this afternoon. "Howdy," he finally said, glancing up at the intruder.

"Smoking!" the man said. "And at your age!"

"Naw."

"You certainly were!"

Lee shrugged. He was so tired of strangers and other adults who seemed to feel that they had warrant to criticize him whenever they wished. "Anyway, I only had two."

"But why are you out here all by yourself when you should be…"

Lee waited for the rest of the question, which, however, never came. Down below, the breams were now merely toying with his bait, nudging it with their snouts. The very last he wanted was for the man to come and sit next to him on shore, which is what he now did, unconcerned, apparently, as to what it might do to his expensive-looking clothes. His tie was blue in color and covered with dots, and his wristwatch, Lee attested, had four hands on it rotating at various speeds. Nor had his fine suit been designed to be worn in a forest—of that much Lee was certain. A minute now crept by as both men studied the flotation device that Lee had rigged to the line.

"Perhaps they don't care for it," the man offered. "Might it not perhaps be better to use some other form of bait?"

Lee said nothing.

"What *are* you using?"

"Crickets."

"Ah! So there's your problem right there."

Far away, near to the opposite shore, a turtle of some sort had clambered out onto a little island of about the size of a hat and sat there, staring back at them stigmatically. The sun, it is true, had fallen into the limbs of the pines, allowing Lee to perceive bits and pieces of it, but not the whole sphere. He no longer expected to catch any further breams, not with an adult sitting next to him while commenting every few seconds about something or another. Gathering his things, the child made ready to leave.

"Think I'll try it over *there*," he said courteously, nodding toward a location some distance away.

"Very well."

"Anyway, you don't have to come."

"Oh Lee, Lee, Lee. I think you should come with *me*, no? I know of a far better place than this."

"Sir?"

"Why, yes. Where the prey is larger, and the depths so much deeper. Does that appeal to you, I wonder?"

"Well, how much bigger are they?"

The man laughed out loud. He had a significant number of fillings in his otherwise healthy-looking and well-distributed teeth. He was also wealthy, Lee speculated, and his book bore a cover of brown cloth with a rubricated title on it. His glasses were thick, one lens tinted and the other clear, the two having obviously been ground to very different prescriptions. Finally, to reckon from his head of hair, which was filigreed with silver, the man must have been almost thirty or forty years old.

"Enormous, Lee, grander than the world. And don't you think it's time, really, to seek after other things than breams? How old are we now?"

"Thirteen. But I'll be fourteen in eight and a half months."

"Fourteen! Life is running out for you, Lee, and now has come the time for you to hurry." He stood painfully and dusted himself off, giving special attention to the seat of his trousers. "Come, if you wish. Or not."

He followed at a distance. His father's farm was far behind and they were traveling across uneven country beset with hills and creek beds, most of them dry. Never would he have supposed that a smiling city person could know these complicated trails so well. Nor was it easy to stay with the man, who was taller than average and, unlike Lee, had brought no fishing tackle with him, nor a string of still-breathing fish. Looking forward eagerly to the lake he had been promised, the boy managed at that moment to tangle his hook in one of the overhanging branches, forcing him to come to a halt.

"Yes?" asked the man, turning and looking back with the first evidence of displeasure that Lee had so far seen in him. "Why are you standing there like that?"

"Aw, it's just the hook." Lee pointed to it. "It's caught."

The man groaned and glanced briefly to heaven. He would not come back and give aid to Lee, not until he had finished the page he was reading and had selected a leaf of grass with which to mark his place. The child recognized now that the man had been reading all this time, even while marching at high speed along the path. It also startled him when the man chose simply to break the line apart, leaving the hook out of reach.

"Hey!" Lee said. "What about my hook?"

"It shall be dark in two hours—do you prefer to spend the night here, or in the place to which we are going?"

"I don't know," Lee said honestly. "I thought we was going to a *lake*. You said."

"I also recommend that you leave those... *creatures* here by the roadside, where the wildlife can have them."

"They're breams!"

"Possibly so, but you could move so much faster without them. Now Lee, we're coming close to the highway and it wouldn't be good if anyone saw us."

They went on.

It seemed to Lee they had traversed half of Alabama when they came upon an abandoned farmstead in the very late afternoon, a vacant space where the county's last surviving windmill, driven to extremes by old age, had made a final bow and plunged its face into the sand. They surveyed the scene, both of them striving to reconstruct in imagination the family and children and the generations of mules that once had graced this half-acre. Lee, who knew a great deal more about such matters than did the city man, espied the remains of a scuppernong arbor that lay against a ruined shack with a curled tin roof.

"He's going to call the sheriff, my daddy is, if I'm not home before suppertime."

"Yes."

"Anyway, I don't even think there *is* any lake." He was close to tears. "And besides, I'm gettin' tired!"

"Yes, 'tired.' But remember this, Lee... It *is* 'Lee?'"

"Yes, sir."

"Remember the Ten Thousand, Lee, and the tiredness *they* must have felt, staggering into Sinope on that day. Let it give you pause, child. After all, they were *many* more miles from home than you."

Lee now began to cry. His sobs, which he tried to contain, served only to make his cigarette brighter and this, in turn, gave away his location. The man, too, was saddened by it.

"Yes, cry—I won't tell. It's hard, I know it is. And I wish there were some other way, truly I do."

"Me too, that's what I wish, too."

"Ten days, Lee — that's all it needs. And the crying will be over."

"No it won't."

"Here, I'll strike a match. And then you can light up again!"

And did so. Already he had had more cigarettes than he wanted, and his head was not well. No supper. *And* he needed to pee.

Twilight, when it came, came quickly as they moved into the hills that converged upon the town called Pleuron, an important place formerly, now reduced to some half-hundred homes, most of them empty. They passed on tiptoes, moving as quietly as possible between the splayed legs of the enormous water tower, famous in the region for the malicious-looking face painted on the tank itself. For twenty years and more, that visage had been grinning down into the valley, blighting crops, intimidating farmers, and causing more than the ordinary number of wives to go without child.

The town itself had slumbered off to sleep, leaving two bored hounds to yap all night and bother peoples' dreams. Squinting into the murk, Lee was able to make out an almost invisible wisp of smoke lifting daintily from the vestigial volcano called "Epsilon," a bloated hump that sat askew on the horizon at a distance of about three days to the north-northeast.

"What see you there, lad?" He pointed to the village with both hands. "Speak."

"Pleuron?"

"Nay, lad; we left that near two hours ago."

"Worm Rood?"

"And so you've been reduced to guessing. That hurts. Ten hours on the trail and already your little mental map has given out entirely."

But Lee was not as much troubled by that as by his knowledge of the commotion that would have broken out by now among his parents and neighbors, and among the sheriff, too, who had been disturbed once before by events pertaining to something that Lee had done. But even that faded into inconsequentiality when compared to what was happening now, miles from home, in steep terrain, with the dew so dense Lee felt as if he were wading through spit.

"I'm tired! And my socks is all wet, too!"

"*Are* all wet."

The moon, when it came, came up greenly. To Lee it looked like a balloon making its escape from a devastated child, still leaping for the string. Lee had long ago taken over the leadership of their two-person column, and several times had had to endure the man stepping on his heel.

"Tarnation!"

"Sorry."

"*Now* which way?"

"Hm? East, go east."

"It's too steep!"

"Oh, not really."

Together they darted across the highway. The hour was dark, and in any case, Lee had lost hope of being noticed by any of the wagon drivers or occasional automobiles. His tackle box was a heavy inconvenience, and in the meantime, the smaller of his two breams had dropped off when he wasn't looking. He was tired, his cigarettes were mostly gone, and he needed to urinate even more urgently than before. That was when the man stepped forward and rested his hand on Lee's right shoulder.

"We'll wait here. It won't be long."

"What won't?"

"Oh dear, here comes an automobile."

They drew deeper into the woods, making themselves invisible among the undergrowth. The car itself was coming on so slowly that at one moment Lee thought of breaking free and trying to leap on board the vehicle, but changed his mind when he realized that the man had taken a firmer grasp on his belt.

"Don't even think of it, Lee."

"No, sir."

"Because you'd never forgive yourself."

Lee said nothing. He'd always been able to forgive himself in the past. "Yes, sir."

"Anyway, you don't want to ride with a fellow that looks like that."

The driver now passed slowly in front of their eyes, a sleepy-looking individual whose arm hung out. They watched as the car continued on for another few hundred yards before then turning off toward Calera, as Lee supposed. Waiting in place, he gathered two or three blackberries that grew within reach, sweet ones scintillating in the moon. The man laughed at him.

"Yes! You're an autochthonous boy, a native son. We can make use of you, Lee, in the place to which we are going."

It was Lee's first indication that he was not to be killed.

"Well, where *are* we going—that's what I want to know! Shoot, I don't even think there *is* any lake!" He blushed, suddenly ashamed for having doubted the word of an adult. "All right, I guess there's a lake all right."

"Well, certainly."

"But I never would of come in the first place, if I'd knowed how far..."

"Hush. Here comes the bus."

Later on, thinking back upon it, he was to remember his surprise that of the fifteen or so persons on board that bus, all, save the driver, were of his own general type and size, all of them gazing straight forward. He fixed upon a boy in a brown cap who sat near the rear, a cynical-looking type with scuff marks on him whom Lee immediately disliked—they looked at each other coldly. Based upon early impressions, Lee believed that he could thrash most of the people there, even while admitting that two or three could probably thrash *him*. Quickly he reached for a cigarette, igniting it in open view while wearing a craggy expression on his face.

His second surprise came when his abductor ushered him down the aisle and then pressed him to sit next to a certain little blond-headed boy, stained with tears.

"Well!" the man said. "And so we part. Perhaps we'll meet again someday, my friend. Well, no, probably not, to be absolutely truthful about it." They shook. Lee, with his bream in his lap and his fishing pole scratching at the ceiling, tried to return the man's grasp, which was friendly and strong. "You'll go far, I think."

"Doubt it. I never even wanted to go this far." He turned to see if the boy in the brown cap was listening.

The man laughed merrily, and then turned and abandoned the bus, pausing briefly to give a few words to the driver. The vehicle was noisy and old and gave off a good deal of smoke as it began moving forward once again. Lee found himself gazing straight ahead, unwilling to break the pattern the other boys had established. Had they been ordered not to speak among themselves? Judging from it, Lee was inclined to believe that they had.

They drove in silence for the next twenty minutes. At one moment, Lee caught sight of a grist mill that seemed familiar to him—until he viewed it in more detail and perceived that it was being used for hay.

Except for that, the countryside offered very few landmarks to guide him home again. He did catch sight of a series of little advertising signs set up at a distance from one another, each subsequent sign providing one more line of poetry in praise of a certain after-shave lotion. It was while he was reading these that he chanced to view the face of the boy sitting just next to him, a pale one in a blue shirt, his eyes hollowed out from too much crying.

"Howdy," Lee said very quietly, minimizing his lip movements. No one watching from more than ten or fifteen feet away could have known that he was actually speaking. He had to wait a long time for the reply:

"Hi."

"Where we going?"

"We don't know." And then: "We're not supposed to talk."

"How come?"

"Ssssh!"

Lee looked at him. He had seen people of this type — blond hair, delicate, thin arms sticking out of short sleeves that were too large for the boy's actual size. He had been crying to such an extent that his eyes had gone dead and his tears had turned to sand. Next Lee looked to the driver, an ordinary middle-aged man with an extravagant belly. Shielding his mouth, Lee said this:

"They's just one of him. They's fifteen of us."

"No!"

"How come?"

"Because! Anyway, I… Hey, what's that?"

"Bream."

The boy reached out and touched it. His finger, too, was pale and as delicate as a girl's. "You're must be from Birmingham," Lee guessed. "Are you?"

"No!"

"Where, then?"

"Bahston."

"Oh yeah, I've heard about that. But it's not Bahston, it's Boston. B-O-S…"

"I was just sitting on the stoop!"

"I know it; you just can't trust nobody these days. What's a stoop?"

"He lied, too!"

"I ain't surprised. Nothing surprises me, not these days."

"And where is *this*?" He pointed to the Alabama ground moving past at high speed.

"I'm thinking we're still in Shelby County."

"No, what state?"

"Alabama."

The boy began to cry.

They crossed the county line at just after midnight and then veered off onto an unpaved road where the bus immediately began to throw up a veil of scarlet dust that would need half an hour before it finally settled once again. Clinging to the window—he had transferred to a vacant seat where he could smoke in peace—Lee witnessed the silhouettes of cattle standing about at random, each cow gazing off in its chosen direction. Warm weather it was, and the clouds were black. In the meantime, a locust of some nature had fixed itself to the exterior of the window pane, allowing Lee a close inspection of its nether portions. As to how the thing had found a footing on a surface so smooth, he could not imagine. He saw a silo overflowing at the top, a farmhouse with a gazebo and a lightning rod bent over at the top, Alabama scenes that gave comfort to him in spite of his predicament. The truth was, he knew nothing of the regions that lay to the east of Shelby County, and for all that he could know, they might have crossed over into Georgia by now.

Two

On Tuesday, September 11, young Leland Pefley passed over a single-lane bridge and entered a pleasant-looking valley full of agriculture. With woods on one side and fields on the other, and with a covey of blackbirds watching from the telephone wire, the boy checked his watch to find that it was less than half an hour before midday. There was a lake, jagged about the edges, ten acres worth perhaps, and a scattering of carmine-colored barns, one of them lying on its side. As for Georgia, there was too much kudzu for that, which wasn't even to mention an abandoned car bearing the license plate of his native state. It was here the bus left the open road and began moving carefully through tall grass, the sort of terrain that left no tracks behind. Ahead he saw a complex of unpainted buildings arrayed in higgledy-piggledy fashion beneath an overhanging hill. But Lee's eye was particularly drawn to a two-story structure with a telescope protruding through the roof.

The boys all stood at the same time and filed out into the light, where some half-dozen smiling adults stood waiting to receive them. If he set out running now, he could reach the woods in under a minute, Lee believed. However, encumbered as he was with fishing equipment and a paper cup of dead crickets, he agreed to shake with the man, a tall one with a worn leather satchel, who came forward to greet him.

"Howdy," Lee said, putting on a cordial face.

"Lee?"

"Yes, sir."

"So glad you could make it — we were worried. Did you have a good trip?"

"I guess. Pretty good."

"I don't suppose you've had anything to eat, have you?"

"Yesterday. My mother fixed it. Say, y'all don't have a restroom here, do you?" He took out a cigarette, one of the very few still remaining to him, and lit it on the second attempt.

"I don't believe you've met Dr. Goldman."

Lee stepped forward three paces and shook with a great bald-headed man who seemed to have the authority in this place. Normally he preferred to shake up and down for just two or three strokes; now he was being forced to go on with it for a full ten seconds or more.

"And so *you're* that Leland Pefley person," the man said. "Am I right about that?"

Lee admitted that he was.

"Good, good. Good. We plan to make use of you, you understand. Most of our boys are from Birmingham, Atlanta, places like that."

"Yes, sir. And Boston."

"Why, yes."

"Actually I don't even know why I'm here, sir. Say, y'all don't have a *telephone* do you?"

"Telephone?" He laughed. "Oh, I'm sure you know better than that." Already he was turning his attention to the next boy, a heavy-set type in wide pants and milky lenses set in a mahogany frame. Lee stood by as Dr. Goldman tried to calm the boy, even going so far as to get down painfully on one knee and speak to him on his own level, as it were.

They were ushered down a narrow lane bordered on both sides with pastel-colored cottages supported on stilts — the terrain was that uneven — their exteriors decorated with landscape scenes. Lee marched straight ahead, striving to show with his facial expression that he had been abducted, in the event someone might be watching from the homes. He saw a middle-aged woman who had come out onto her porch in order to sprinkle — Lee now, more than ever, wanted to pee — sprinkle the numerous potted plants that dangled from the crossbeam. He caught a glimpse of the lake sparkling through the trees, and then a long, narrow building that had served as a warehouse in the old days, judging from the almost imperceptible inscription that ran around the architrave.

"We still in Shelby County?" he asked the man marching at his side, an elderly person whose face reminded Lee somewhat of a skink's.

"Nay, lad; you're still thinking in linear terms. We'll have to cure you of that."

"Yes, sir."

"Teach you to think in *abstractions* — suppose you'll like that?"

"Doubt it."

"No?"

"But I'm willing to give it a try," Lee quickly amended.

The building was older and in worse condition than he knew. He stood aside as Goldman dithered with the lock and then finally managed to open the door. It was dark in there, and the place was suffused with the smell of peanut hulls and linseed oil. Lee, led forward by Goldman, the bus driver, and the boy in the brown cap, entered cautiously, finding that he was in a hallway that ran the length of the building and came out on the other side. He waited for his sight to adjust and to confirm that some dozen little chambers, one with a boy in it, opened onto the corridor in the style of a hotel. His spirits sank, Lee's did, although he had always known in his heart that it must, sooner or later, come to something like this.

"And I only smoked *one* pack. One!"

"Aren't you lucky! See? You can have your choice of rooms."

They continued down the corridor, Goldman blocking off all hope of escape. Each cell had at least one desk and one bed in it, whereas the carpeting, such as it was, was worn down to the very planks, such as they were, too. He started to say something about that, but then chose instead to move on to the next compartment, where a small boy sat on his cot with a valise in his lap and a number of personal possessions spread out around him.

"Burt?"

"Sir?"

"You're not still crying!"

"Yes, sir."

"I want you to meet Leland."

They looked at one another. It did Lee good to see that the boy was smaller than himself, and more afraid. Offering to shake with him, Lee still had to wait a considerable time before the boy could take all the things out of his lap, climb down from the cot, and then come forward.

"Howdy. I'm Leland."

"I know."

They shook.

"I used to live pretty near here," Lee said, pointing around to where he believed he used to live. "Not *real* near; *pretty* near."

"I'm from Jersey."

"We used to have some jerseys. Sold 'em."

"What are they going to do to us, Leland?"

Lee glanced at Goldman, who seemed to be enjoying this.

"I don't know. Kill us, I reckon."

"Why!"

"I don't know. They just like it, I guess."

In the end, it was the man who selected the room, a square space about ten feet long and eight feet high that provided a superior view of the woods and lake. Bare, poorly furnished, and with no wallpaper, he had seen better than this in the homes of the negroes who worked his father's land.

"Yes, it's austere. But you'll make it livable, I'm sure, over the process of time. Here, see? This is an ideal place to store your rod and bait."

"Process of time?"

"Exactly."

"Well, how much time do I got — that's what I want to know?"

"Before we kill you, you mean?" He laughed richly. "About seventy years, I estimate. Longer, if you stay away from cigarettes."

Seventy years in a narrow cell — Lee was not so sure, but that he might prefer to die.

"And now I must leave you. But let me recommend this, Lee — that you spend the next hours reflecting back over your past life up until this point. Will you do that? For, unlike Burt, you've brought no private belongings to spread out around you and remind you of home."

Lee nodded. He was willing to let the man believe that his advice was being taken seriously.

"Your own past life. It shouldn't take long, not with as little past life as you've had up until this point. And then come outside, do, and explore your new surroundings!"

In point of fact, he spent less than a quarter of an hour thinking over his past activities, at the end of which time he arose and positioned his cup of crickets next to a few boring-looking old books leaning up against one another on the second-topmost shelf of the floor-to-ceiling cabinet that took up most of one wall. His pole, on the other hand, was too tall to be so easily stored, so he broke it down into its constituent sections and propped them in a corner of the closet. Apart from that, the room had a cot, a brick-lined fireplace with a tiny capacity, and a long, low, level desk in bad condition that was nearly as large as the door. The carpet itself was old and exhausted, and had worn down to the weave. He was accustomed to a chest of drawers with clothes and letters and a stamp collection in it, not to mention model airplanes hanging from the ceiling by cords; here he had a bedpan peeping out from beneath the cot and some half-rick of firewood stacked haphazardly in the corner.

It was past three in the afternoon when he finally ventured out into the hall and began to inspect the other kidnapped boys in greater detail. Almost every room had a boy in it and almost every boy was sitting at his desk, gazing out at the lake and hills. He tapped twice at the door of a thin individual in a uniform of some kind and then, getting no acknowledgment from him, passed on to a rangy, raw-boned sort of fellow who whistled as he unloaded his suitcase.

"Howdy," Lee said, holding out his hand. "Where are *you* from? Naw, I was just asking."

The boy turned on him, his eyes shining with anger. "Shit, I don't know! Shit, I was just coming back from town when that big son-of-a-bitch… Hey, who do they think they am?"

"Criminals, is what they are."

"Well sure they're criminals! Everybody knows that. You don't have to tell me they're criminals! Shit, I knew that as soon as they put me in that truck!" He went back to whistling. Lee was amazed at the possessions that flowed from his suitcase, tools mostly, including a brace-and-bit and several screwdrivers of various sizes. Finally, having cooled somewhat, the boy asked this:

"What about you — where you from?"

"Well, I..."

"Never mind, I don't even want to know. It ain't got nothing to do with me."

"Bibb County."

"Yeah, but what town — that's what *I* was asking."

"Blafusia." He tried to keep his pride from showing.

"Blafusia, my ass! Hey, you don't know a nigger down there called *Willy P.*, do you?"

Lee searched his inventory. "I guess not."

"That son-of-a-bitch's got some of the best hunting dogs I ever seen in my life! Shit, I started to buy one."

"We got a farm down there, my father and us. Four hundred acres, near about."

"I didn't ask about that! Anyhow, cotton ain't worth shit this year."

That was true.

"Well, I just wanted to see how you were making out," said Lee, bringing matters to a close.

"Not worth a shit."

"Me neither."

They shook again and Leland left.

He persisted in his narrow room for another half-hour, wasting the day arranging and rearranging the few scant pieces of furniture that had been provided to him. His cot was an especially poor sort of thing, a mere skein of canvas with a breadth of perhaps eighteen inches. His desk, on the other hand, was solid enough to hold his weight, and enabled him to exit the room by way of the window.

In the village, smoke lifted languorously from two of the cottages and went tumbling skyward, simulating secret codes. Directing himself toward the lake, he moved as slowly as he dared, hoping in this way to ward off any unwanted notice from the adults. A man on a bicycle waved to him in a friendly way, and Lee immediately waved back. A woman in a garden was giving too much attention to her squashes to pay any regard to him. All about him were hills, their likenesses so reliably reflected in the lake that they seemed to offer alternate routes to conduct him home again. His job now was simply to move along the shore, pausing from time to time till the moment came to make his escape. This much he knew for certain — that once he was inside those trees, no living man could hope to find him.

And that, of course, was when he detected a man who *might* be living, but in any case was old, an old man in an antique sweater coming toward him with a basket on his arm. Lee's tactic was to smile endearingly and, as a measure of respect, to doff the cap that, in fact, he had left behind today. In lieu of the cap, Lee smiled again and held the expression.

"Don't even think about it, Lee."

"Sir?"

"Running off into the trees. It won't succeed."

They drew even. Within the man's basket, Lee saw a number of things, but especially a half-eaten apple, a vacated turtle shell, a set of field glasses, and a thin book with so many blades of grass used as bookmarks that it looked as if the man had sown seeds there the previous spring. Both men stepped back somewhat and continued studying each other, up and down. Of Lee there was little enough, whereas of the old man there was also a good deal less than one might have originally supposed. Lee could have outrun him and out-jumped him and could have swum much further, too — these were his thoughts. Instead, at that moment, the old man reached into his basket and tenderly drew out one of the very thinnest slices of grey shale that Lee had recently seen.

"Ah, Lee" he said, "those dark times so long ago. See where the little darlings have turned to stone?"

But Lee continued to stare at the person. He was too old and naïve and his eyes too poor to give chase. Just now he was pointing out with his pen certain almost imperceptible striations in the face of the slate.

"Scales and teeth, teeth and scales—that's what passed for progress in those days. And how would *you* like it, Leland, to pass your whole life creeping along forlornly at the bottom of the sea?"

"Naw."

"The insecurity! Tsk, tsk, tsk. Your great invertebrates, acolytes of the brand-new sun. But all that was as nothing, Lee, when compared to what was occurring on dry land."

"What?"

"Just awful." And then, in a voice that was soft and low and highly confidential: "Don't do it, Lee—force us to chase you down in our busy season. I won't even mention the certainty of your failure. We have dogs."

"Look, I don't even know why…!"

"Yes, it's horribly unfair; we acknowledge that. What, thirteen? Fourteen? It's true that I wouldn't much care for you if you didn't try at least one time to get back home again. But not in our busy season, please!"

Lee, too disorganized to run, continued to stare, sometimes into the man's beet-red face, sometimes the basket, and at least once at the page of slate to which the man continued to point with death-like patience, using his ballpoint pen for that function.

"And now I recommend you toddle on back to your quarters, Lee, to devote the next hour to thinking back over your own past life and errors."

"I've already done that!"

"Of course you have! But have you done it to the degree that your old life is finished and your errors done with, ah?"

Already they were halfway back to the settlement, the man leading him on with talk and fossils. They only halted once, so that the man might chase down a mollusk of some sort being pushed further and further ashore by successive waves.

"Seventy million years and still wiggling! Do you think you'll like that, Lee? Geology classes?"

"Doubt it."

Just then one of the ganders stood up on the lake and began churning and lifting itself, and then finally flying off toward a defile in the hills, all of it greatly pleasing the man.

"These autumn fogs! Time to gather ye hoard of firewood, Lee, lest it be too late... For when winter comes—and it's always the same—it will be full of horrors for the old *and* the young."

"Hoard?"

"Well, now, here are your quarters. I suggest you run to them, that's right, and spend the next minutes thinking back over..."

Lee groaned. His cigarette had burned down, leaving him with nothing to do but fling it away.

He was at his desk, absolutely refusing to think back over his own past when the Director and another man entered the room and circled him several times, inspecting the boy from various angles. It angered Lee to have his head twisted this way and that, and by a hand that was not very gentle.

"He *does* have the bony structure."

The other man, a thin individual wearing a yellow jacket and matching visor, wrote it down on his clipboard.

"But oh my Lord, the ignorance. See that? Makes me tired to look at you, boy."

"Yeah, but I never even...!"

"Quiet!" said the second man, his voice hoarse with indignation. "Don't you see that Mr. Goldman is speaking?"

"And has he thought over his own past and finally dispensed with it? Apparently not."

Instead of answering, Lee fixed his attention upon the man himself. He had seen the type before—a large man with an opaline complexion and a massive head containing two glittering eyes that sat much too close to each other on either side of a nose that was much too thin.

"Nor firewood. Why, he hasn't brought in a single stick! You'd rather freeze than to study knowledge—is that how it is?"

"Look, all I ever...!"

"And so you just sit there while Mr. Goldman has to go on standing. By golly, that makes my dander rise!"

Lee leapt up, whereupon the Director took his place. Outside, an automobile had arrived, releasing yet one more thirteen- or fourteen-year-old brought from the outer world. Lee estimated that the building now held a good two dozen of them at least, and perhaps even more. Seeing that Lee had turned his attention to the new boy (trying incompetently to escape), Goldman said this:

"Don't look at *him*—he doesn't operate this place—look at *me* when someone is talking."

"Yes, sir." The new boy had gone only a brief distance before finding his path blocked by the lake.

"*Three hundred thousand green dollar bills American*—that's what it takes in order to turn someone with a bony structure like yours. And so we tend to take it amiss, Leland, when someone tries to run off into the hills."

"We have dogs," the second party said.

"My pore granddaddy, he'd piddle all over hisself if he could see how we squander his estate. Squandering it on *you*."

"Yeah, but…!"

"You don't imagine it comes free, do you? The lake and hills, the library and the observatory behind it. You don't imagine that all that came to be here without someone having to pay for it, do you?"

"Observatory?"

"Oh my gracious, I didn't think you'd do that Lee, I really didn't—make a comment like that. All right, the observatory isn't finished yet—we admit that. What, you need to piss?"

For twenty hours, Lee had needed to piss. Goldman, lost in thought, continued:

"Three hundred thousand. Green bills. Yes, you're a hard case, Lee, everybody knows that. But we'll fix your wagon, just you wait and see!" He tried to rise, a project that required all three men. Lee was left standing face-to-face with the other party, whose features were as specific to him as Goldman's to his.

"You do understand how to read books, do you not?"

"I guess. Anyhow, it's just a bunch of hooey, most of it."

The man exclaimed aloud and then slowly lifted his glasses, and with his eyes squeezed tight, began to knead the narrow of his already too narrow nose.

"All right, good, yes, very well. Now Lee, this is a book. See it?"

He was holding the thing directly under the boy's nose, as if he wanted him to sniff of it. The book had limp covers and tended to drop open, exposing some of the interior.

"Yes, sir. Book."

"Good. And by tomorrow, you will have read the first twenty pages, no?"

Lee took it. It was heavy enough, and had a look to it that put him in mind of all other blue, boring books the world over.

Night did come. Thinking back upon it at a much later time, he was to remember only that night *had* come, that he was at the lake, that a bonfire was blazing brightly on shore, and that he and some twenty-six other boys had formed into a circle where they sat, entranced and silent. It almost seemed to Lee, owing to the highly detailed reflections produced by the flames, as if the lake were also burning. Thus some minutes went by in silence, until a fat man in a bathrobe rose up from the group and, lifting both arms, began the invocation:

"Met a stranger from an antique land, etcetera."

The boys looked about at each other.

"Went to Washington, yes I did. Craved to see the Howard Hansom Tower, the Poe complex, Faulkner Center. Walked for miles, I did, and yet — and need I say it? — all that I could ever see were inscribed to *public* men!"

Lee, moving like a crawfish, broached nearer to the fire. He had identified the speaker's wife, he believed, based upon the way she sat staring up at him, her mouth dangling open in admiration.

"Boys, boys. Read widely, boys, but especially read these hills!" He pointed to them, pointing at their reflection in the lake. "For here, boys, among us, the Lord of Beauty has overthrown all other gods and scattered them far!"

"Crazy," someone whispered. Indeed, there was a restlessness in the crowd. Lee locked glances with the same red-headed boy he had first seen on the bus, a raw-looking person, his face printed with contempt. Right away, Lee saw that this was not, and never had been, a good person. He held his own facial expression in reserve, waiting upon events. The man went on speaking:

"Wished to visit the Parkman Museum, yes I did. And found it, too. Boys, boys. The place has been renamed for a moneyed man!"

A groan went up.

"Remember, boys, that of all the places there are, all of them, *all*, have set course on the pragmatic trajectory, all save here. I ask you!"

"What?"

It was a small boy who asked — an earnest type, judging from his looks — who had recently been crying a great deal.

"Remember! We cannot do it for the whole world, therefore we do it for thee! And if you hate us now, soon you'll hate us, ah, so much more!

So forget now your childish pleasures, do, and tonight, with your tears, wash them all away. And tomorrow—ah, tomorrow!—tomorrow we begin to move to those *higher* joys. Geometry, I mean."

A moan went up. Lee was focused upon two fireflies who appeared to be dueling each other a few inches above the surface of the lake. And saw one of them go swimming off at high speed, its lantern quenched. The man was continuing:

"That's right—geometry. And poetry and philosophy, too. Oh! More of poetry than you thought your poor little heads could hold! Music! Music, botany, and Chinese. Who can throw the javelin best? We want no boy here who can't run to Slocum's Corner and back again in under ten minutes. Chess!"

"And not one single girl."

"Yes, no girls. This is a *thinking place*, my friends."

The man now returned to his wife, who received him with delight. The following speaker was a tall man with four or five days' growth of beard whom Lee at first viewed as a pioneer or cowboy, or something in that line. Now, holding aloft a knurled staff of about six feet in length, he waited for the crowd to recover from what they had just been told. Finally:

"Disperse now to your sleeping places, and do not speak to one another. And don't imagine that you'll be forming friendships here; there'll be no time for that, and besides, we won't have it. And so I bid you good night."

Lee rose unsteadily and headed off, initially in the wrong direction. In spite of the instructions they'd been given, he could hear one or two of the boys whispering among themselves. Behind him, the fire had collapsed upon itself, rendering the lake gaudier than ever, a vermillion field punctuated with flares and stars. Not for thirty hours had Lee tasted of any sort of food whatsoever, and he could hear a "baseball game" inside his belly, along with the sound of cheering from the bleachers.

Attracted by the sight of the mountains and the dark night, Lee was the tardiest of all the boys in getting back to the dormitory. Entering with prudence, he moved slowly down the hall, unwilling to peep in upon his various colleagues in their cells. A certain amount of loud talk was going on in some of the rooms, and yet the boy in the cell just next to his had already taken up his assigned reading and was applying himself with concentration, as it appeared. Too agitated to read, Lee went directly to the ghastly little hole-in-the-floor that had been provided in lieu of any authentic porcelain toilet, and proceeded to urinate at such extraordinary length that he finally called a halt to it and went back to his quarters. He knew this much already, that he did not want to be an improved person, to live a life without speaking, or to spend his days shut away forever with nothing but a few blue and brown boring books to gaze upon.

He returned to his desk at 9:15 and wasted a quarter of an hour sketching out a letter to his parents in which he tried to describe everything from this most unsettling of all days. He knew, of course, how unlikely it was that he'd be allowed to post it. Nor had he thought to bring a stamp.

The cot was no good, there was too much noise coming from the great room and Lee, just as he had expected, wasn't able to sleep. Going to the window, he saw a powerful beam of light arising from some distant city, scanning frantically for vagrant airplanes, and behind that a ridge of hills that loomed over the community like an ocean-going wave held in suspension for the past ten thousand years. He could hear owls and crickets, cicadas and coyotes, and the scream of a faraway train racing off toward Tennessee. Pressing at the window, he then caught his best sight of the night — of a smiling toad riding past astride a bat.

Making no sound, he opened the window, dropped to the grass and rolled forward a few inches. Would he survive long enough to reach the line of trees? Or the bullet that would kill him — was it even now chasing up behind him at high speed? No, he thought not, not in the absence of warning shouts or the noise of gunshots. The truth was, he had always wanted it to be like this — to be continually escaping out of the grasp of adults who were too large and too heavy, too stupid and too awkward to catch him. His arrogance increased. Finally, coming to within a very short sprint of the forest, he stopped, turned, and bowed sweepingly in the direction of the academy. The last thing he expected was to happen onto another person at this juncture, a small one, from Boston, huddled in the weeds. Lee jumped back in great surprise, but then managed to bring himself under control.

"Thought I'd go for a little walk," he said calmly, taking out a cigarette and lighting it in a leisurely fashion.

"Me, too; I'm going, too."

"Get the lay of the land. Look around a little bit."

"Yeah! See what it looks like."

"Right."

"Besides," Lee attested, "I don't even think they've got any dogs."

"Dogs!"

"Anyhow, they can't catch us now. Shoot, we can go home, if we want to."

"Yeah!" And then in a lower voice: "We aren't supposed to be talking to each other. He said."

Lee lit another match and brought it up to the boy's face. His case was even more severe than Lee's, nor would he come out of hiding.

"You can stay with me," Lee now volunteered.

The boy brightened. "I can?"

"Sure. Two or three days."

"Oh."

"Until we can get the sheriff after that ole… Goldfart."

"Yeah!" He emerged from his nest.

"He'll *kill* him, ain't no doubt about it," Lee said.

They grinned wildly at one another. The night was warm and the fireflies, few and far apart, had to signal with special effort to cover the distances. Just then a terrible noise disturbed the stillness. The other boy, called "Burcham," or "Edmund Burchem," or called sometimes "Young Edmund," or "Young Burcham," screamed. In the meantime, Lee had ignited a second cigarette and was in the process of offering it to the boy who, however, wanted nothing to do with it.

"What's that!"

"Tree frog."

"And…?"

"That? Coyote."

"Oh God."

They went on.

It took them until past midnight to come to the top of the hill. From that position, Lee was able to make out the expanses that awaited them, a broad region, dark and green and so dense with pines and other things that he was not absolutely confident of being able to squeeze between them. And then, too, he had this second boy with him, who tended to hold back and to spend most of his time protecting his eyes from the twigs and branches that came to meet them. He had more dread of snakes, apparently, than of Goldman.

"I tell you what," Lee finally said, "you wait here and I'll…"

"No!"

"…fetch the sheriff."

"No, no, no, no, no! Just *no*, OK? It's bad."

Lee looked at him. In the moon, his face looked like a pool of milk with dark spots on it. And although he had finally agreed to take the cigarette, he still only blew on it rather than inhaling. As to how Leland's ancestors, riflemen, had arranged to forfeit a war against *these* people, stoop sitters… It was a mystery.

"Want to go back?"

"OK!"

"Thought so. Well, gimme the goddamn cigarette then, if you ain't going to use it."

"Hey! Aren't you coming, too?"

"Well, shoot, no, I'm not coming! I'm going *home.*"

The boy began to cry.

Lee cursed and insulted the boy, but finally did agree to convey him back to the institution. Thus far there had been no indication of dogs — save only for one far-away yelp that seemed to come from miles away. Across the pond, a lamp came on briefly in one of the homes before soon going out again. Was this one of the guards, or even Goldman himself suffering from dreams of guilt? Lee liked to think so.

Three

He dreamt throughout the night that he was sleeping and was chagrined when morning came. Having expected to awaken in his father's house, he lay in a state of some confusion at first, which is to say until he had been able to remember his past life leading up to this moment. Lying on his narrow cot, he saw the sun come up tentatively behind the trees, loiter there briefly, and then vanish behind the horizon once again. The true dawn, when it came, would be much more powerful than that. In the meantime he began to hear roosters and automobiles and the other usual precursors of a brand new day. Five minutes more having gone by, he forced himself out of bed and had drained off a significant portion of his chambered bladder when he heard what sounded like an adult pounding on the door:

"Six o'clock!"

"Yes, sir!"

By the time he got outside, some two score of boys, more or less, had formed up in order of promptitude and stood at attention in front of the gaunt-looking individual — a farmer, Lee at first imagined — who was responsible for having awoken them. Grey and long, the man's beard appeared to be entangled in his tie. Immediately Lee went and fell in next to Young Edmund, whose shirt was wrongly buttoned, whose hair was not combed, and who had gone all night, apparently, without any sleep at all.

"Look, you," said the man. He was pointing at the dawn, a blue and yellow manifestation that looked as if some enormous child had splashed one can after another of bright, vivid paint against the sky. "My advice is to look at it afresh each morning, as if dawn had never been seen before, or not by you at any rate, and perhaps not even by others!" He smiled, musing upon his words. "To be sure, you must look for it, morning, at morning time; otherwise it's nearly always gone!"

The boys groaned. Here was the maddest man yet in this whole mad valley, and his words the most irrational that Lee had yet heard. They exchanged glances, Edmund and Lee and a third person in a baseball cap. There were fumes coming off the lake, a propitious circumstance for perch and small-mouth bass. Smoke also lapped the hills, admixed with fog and clouds. From somewhere Leland detected the smell of bacon and coffee, sent forward on the rooster's call.

Following the man, they jogged downhill in a crowd, threading their way conscientiously between the gardens and cantilevered houses scattered seemingly at random up and down the slope. Rarely had Lee observed a dew as dense as this, a pearl-colored exudation already beginning to blow off in the mild heat of early morning. Where were they going? He saw no particular building before them. They were going toward the lake.

It was a brick-made dam, twenty feet high, that held the pond in place. Each separate brick, Lee noted with surprise, bore his grandfather's trademark of six small and large candles profiled in the sun. Here, where no doubt the depth was at its deepest, some half-dozen women were tarrying on shore with clipboards and frying pans and, in the case of one woman especially, a bundle of clean, white towels lapping her arm. To them the man addressed a word or two and then, turning to the boys, enunciated in a low voice the most dismaying of all possible commands:

"Off with your clothes."

A shout went up and Edmund began to cry. To get nude in front of women...! Lee looked for, and thought that he could see, an opening in the trees.

"No, no, you can keep your underwear. Don't worry about the girls — they've seen far better than you. Hurry, hurry!"

One by one, bitterly, the boys untied their laces, removed their shoes, and stood, pale and shivering, along the eastern coast. By now the sun had climbed into the sky and had lost its color.

"See that island?" the man asked.

There *was* an island, a wee one located about three hundred rods from shore.

"And those magnolia flowers?"

There *were* blossoms, possibly of magnolia.

"Now listen to this: the first fifteen boys who fetch me back a magnolia blossom, those boys get breakfast."

"But...!"

"The others? We'll let them wash dishes."

They all looked around at each other, Burcham, Pefley, the others, also a certain flaxen-headed boy who already somewhat worried Lee, a calm-looking type who wore thin glasses that were especially well-kept, sparkling and bright.

"But…!"

"I shan't tell you again."

They still looked around at each other. The woman with the clip-board had taken up her pencil and was prepared to use it, assuming that anyone did anything worth marking down. The calm boy had turned his back and was undressing slowly, forgetting not to remove his glasses and insert them for safekeeping deep within his shoe.

Later on, Lee was to recollect the five or six boys who had no knowledge of swimming, or else had determined not to disrobe, not even partially, in front of women. As for himself, Lee sped out of his clothes, but then wasted more time than he had saved by folding each separate garment in his fastidious way, smoothing it out and laying it straight. And when he at last ran forward and threw himself into the water — cold! — and had progressed a few yards… That was when he realized that he had an ordeal in front of him, a long swim through lily pads and scum and nothing at the end of it but eggs and coffee and, if lucky, perchance a bit of toast with something on it. And yet he found that he was making every exertion within his power, because there was nothing in the world that could motivate him like the dread of doing poorly in front of women and girls.

In fact, he was doing rather well. It occurred to him, based upon what he could see, that although he might not be the first to gather his magnolia, he was not likely to do much worse than fifth or sixth. He despised the confident, perhaps over-confident, way in which the fore-most boy was behaving, an expression of arrogance in which he would sometimes roll over on his back and pull forward in that position. Or was it a strategy for holding some of his strength in reserve?

Lee, who had but small reserves, sped up. Primarily he was worried about the lily pads. The last he wanted at this stage was to become ensnared in the things and drawn down into the bottomless silt to perish miserably, leaving nothing but a question mark next to his name. Suddenly he collided into the red-headed boy, the largest such person in the whole group. This boy had already collected his magnolia wreath, had crowned himself with it, and was well on the way to returning to shore.

Lee went faster. To come sixth or seventh was no disgrace. Arriving at the islet, he clambered up on shore and grabbed one of the flowers, but then almost at once came back and exchanged it for a better one. It surprised him that a considerable number of the boys had given up and simply gone back to shore where they were drying and dressing and casting sullen looks upon those who had not given up, not gone to shore. But all this was as nothing when compared to the boy with the secret reserves of strength. In fact no such reserves had been found and the fellow was floundering badly, and sputtering too, and even calling out for help.

Leland, his endurance at an end, bumped into the coast at the last possible moment and then came out on dry land and crawled theatrically forward where he deposited his flower among the feet of the woman with the clipboard. The good swimmers had gone off to one side where they stood toweling disdainfully — Lee joined them at once — and wearing bored expressions. But as for the best swimmer of them all, a boy whose head was so red and so bullet-shaped that it seemed to have been engineered for cutting through water… That boy had drawn apart even from the other good swimmers.

"I won," he said, snorting. "Won by a mile."

Lee looked at him. It was true that his head was shaped like that. His eyes, however, were too lax and sleepy, and his inch-thick lids too heavy and granulose for Lee to ignore. Two others now came up, seventh- and eighth-place swimmers joined by some lesser people who were conducting themselves more or less befittingly, with eyes cast down. A horse-drawn wagon had come up and parked, bringing with it that smell of coffee and sausage that Lee had first discerned almost half an hour ago.

Until the meal was served, the good swimmers were allowed to return to the water. With dawn finished, and the sun having at last broken the last thread still holding it to the horizon, the lake itself now took on the appearance of molten glass. Suddenly Lee dove deep into the stuff, passing through a level that was nearly purple, or at any rate a shade of blue that looked good enough to drink. A strange morning he had had, and an even stranger yesterday, but nothing could be stranger than this — plain, ordinary water that opened up in front of him and fit more closely than clothes. Again he dove, this time continuing all the way to the floor where he found, not diamonds, but specimens of the local trout, long, brown smiling fellows who at once began to toy with him, knowing as they did that he did not have the slightest chance of catching even the slowest of them. This whole chase was carried out in utter silence. Returning to the surface, he traveled through a pink stratum, tenuous and cold. He could have spent his whole September in this, spinning among layers that differed wildly in tint and flavor; instead the geologist summoned him forth, grinning with approval.

"Ya, ya, splendid isn't it, being young? And how young are we?"

Lee gave his age.

"Good, ya. The great thing, however, is to be splendid when you're *not* young, or even far from young. Think you can manage that?"

"I don't know." He removed himself from the lake.

"That bullet fellow, he beat you by a mile."

But Lee was not given time to reply. One of the inferior swimmers was standing by with a towel, which Lee accepted gracefully. He dried hurriedly and then, using the towel for a skirt, went to join the first-, second-, and fifth-place boys at a twenty-foot-long picnic table set with flowers and cloth napkins together with the bacon and coffee he had deserved. Lee, who had tasted not a bite of food for the past two days, fell upon the stuff, smearing himself about the mouth with albumin and vitelline. He tried, but failed, to wedge an entire slice of toast, which was covered in a marmalade of some type, into his mouth. No one spoke. Hunkered over the table, he drew the stuff nearer to himself. Let just one of those boys try and take anything of his and Lee would stab him with his fork. That was when he observed Young Edmund two tables away, munching with little zest upon a bowl of grits and not much else. The coffee, on the other hand, was good and had a lot of sugar in it.

Ten minutes went by. The wives appeared to be both delighted and appalled by the size and the depth and the quality of their appetites; twice Lee was vouchsafed further coffee and additional fried eggs, vibrant ones that sat tremblingly on his platter while staring up at the sky. Just then, a quarrel broke out at the head of the table, a matter between the bullet-headed boy and a Birminghamian in a short haircut and torn shirt. It passed quickly, however, as soon as a fresh platter of bacon was set in front of them. That was when one of the adults, a tall man who looked like Jefferson Davis, stood up on the bench and began talking:

"Today we swim," he said, "and tomorrow horses. But don't imagine we brought you here for this. Oh no, no, no, your day has just begun.

Hurry now, make haste, and hie you off to that…"—he pointed—"… red-roofed affair you see over yonder where the chimney has broken off and lays lying in the yard."

Led on by the better swimmers, the boys approached the place with caution and then filed inside, passing in front of a smallish man who inspected their profiles, one by one. He was suffering, as it appeared, from a headache, and what he saw in front of him added to his woe.

"My stars. And who might *you* be?"

"Paxton. Sir."

"Ah. You the fellow with the crickets?" Suddenly he seized the boy's left hand and towed him all the way to the board, and after thrusting a stick of chalk upon him, guided his reluctant paw in the creation of what Lee soon was to recognize as the first letter in the Greek alphabet. Disturbed by this style of education, Young Edmund had arisen and gone to the back, and was trying to disguise himself among the several sculptures that sat on individual pedestals in that part of the room. Only the bullet-shaped boy was brash enough to go to the front row, where he sat, chewing on something. The professor now turned his attention to him.

"You!"

The boy smirked.

"Yes, you; you've spent your *whole life* mucking about with reality, haven't you? But now comes the time to forget all that and turn your attention, not to life itself, but to those representations of it embodied in fine literature. Are you the man for that?"

The boy stopped chewing. He did not appear to have understood the question. That was when Lee caught notice of the calm boy, who had thought to bring a pen and paper with him, and a vial of ink. Lee disliked him at once, in large part on account of his glasses. The lenses were too clear, too bright and clean, and were held together in a copper frame. Judging by the thinness of those lenses, it was obvious that the boy needed only the very slightest optical assistance, if any. Lee was further annoyed to see that the fellow was copying down the professor's words in a script in which the letters were all of one size and perfectly spaced. The bullet boy had been sent to the board where he was to waste the next minute trying to draw the one Greek word that they were by now expected to know. Finally the man called a halt to it.

"I am now about to hand out your books to you," he announced. "But first I must take them out of this wooden crate"—there *was* a wooden crate; it sat just next to the desk — "that you've been looking at with so much curiosity."

Lee watched every move, fascinated by how the teacher lifted the books tenderly into the light, as if they were puppies, and he was grieving over their impending dispersal. Lee had changed his mind about the swimming coach and no longer considered that one the oddest man in the valley. Grinning evilly, the professor now opened the first of the volumes and held it up in such a way that the students could see that it did, in fact, have words on every page.

"I am now passing out the books," the man said unnecessarily. "Each scholar gets one."

Lee was just curious enough to break open the cellophane skein that enveloped his personal copy and peep inside it. The stuff was about what he had expected — English words in small type interspersed with an ever smaller in *Greek*, one had to presume. He disliked it at once. Suddenly he glanced over at the boy named "Philip," a cold-looking youth. One would have thought he had mastered the language already, judging by how he scanned through the milk-white pages with a somewhat bored expression. Instead, Lee turned his own attention to the lake, an unpredictable business that tended to change color every few seconds at the behest of the sun. He spotted two swans, a mated pair circling around each other in perfect contentment. Nor was it so late in the year that he couldn't still detect the smell of honeysuckle off the hills. And tonight, weather permitting, he planned to follow that scent all the way home again.

Music lessons were held in what had once been a church of some kind. They entered sullenly, nonplussed by the appearance and dress of the short, bald, fat individual waiting at the altar. Staring up at him, Lee no longer felt that the Greek master was the strangest of them all. Keeping a neutral expression, he sidled up to Young Edmund, who was hiding among the pews. Too depleted to do any further crying at this time, his eyes were as red as coals and his face looked like plaster.

"Well, I guess they're going to kill us now," he said.

"Naw."

"Kill, kill, kill! I knew they would."

"Oh, they are not, neither."

"OK, they're going to *molest* us then."

"Naw, they wouldn't be smartning us up if they was just going to turn around and… What you said. Anyway, I'm leaving."

"Me, too; I'm leaving, too. When are *you* leaving?"

The church was tall, but narrow, and offered plenty of space beneath the pews. The instructor, as Lee now perceived, was both shorter and fatter than he had at first imagined; moreover, with his warts and glove-shaped hands, one of them twitching spasmodically and the other clenched into a fist, he gave the impression of having no patience of any kind. Music filled the hall, making talk impossible. Lee looked for, but failed to find, any wooden crate of books sitting next to the podium.

"No!" the man cried out. "I don't have to endure this—swimming when you were supposed to have been here with me. That one over there, for example—he still looks wet to me!"

He stopped. The music, which was of Leland's least favorite kind, had gathered so much force by now that the man was no longer able to overcome it with his voice. This gave Lee the opportunity to inspect the nearest of the stained-glass windows, a narrow panel illustrating the severed head of a certain well-known prophet lying askance on a golden tray. The adjacent wall had about a dozen portraits on it, including a very turbulent-looking Beethoven, the only one he recognized. Suddenly, a woman—also fat, short, and warted—burst into the room and quickly handed two recordings to her husband before then turning and running back out again. Very gradually, the music began to taper off somewhat, allowing the man to speak.

"Think of it like this," he said, gazing down bemusedly at the audience. "That it wasn't thirteen or fourteen years ago, no, but rather this very morning that you were born. Therefore, let us all now give thanks to the first 10,000 generations of men who endured so much in the way of bad weather, yes, and made so many needful inventions in order that *we*, you and me, yes, that *we*..."—he turned, raising the volume of the music—"that we might..."—higher—"... hear *this*!"

They flinched. It was too much, too loud and had too many notes in it.

"Ha! Don't like it, do you? Well, just remember this, that if you hear me yelling at you, it's simply because of the music—too loud." He stopped and then, fixing his attention upon Philip: "And just what in hell is *that* one—no, not him, the other one—what, I wonder, is he writing down in that pale blue ink? Remember this, that here it's the *will to beauty* that holds sway, nothing else. And so write *that*, if write you must."

Lee was nonplussed. Never had he heard such stuff coming from so fat a man, nor such shrill music tuned so noisily that it threatened the bulbs and panes, the calm boy's lenses, and even the little window in his own tiny wristwatch which Lee now hurriedly covered with his thumb. But all this was as nothing compared to the next movement, when the man began to dance.

"Good!" he said. "And now your rotten little selves are only ninety-nine percent empty. Listen and weep, as Mahler says. And tonight when you try to sleep"—he was grinning evilly—"I believe you'll find my favorite concerto going off every two minutes in your awful, awful little heads!"

In the afternoon, they were herded to the edge of the woods and instructed to sit well apart from each other and, if it proved possible, to nap. For Lee, with his mind constantly contemplating plans of escape, it offered the best chance of the day. Accordingly, he now separated from the others and, after scouting about for a few moments, stationed himself on a good, thick layer of pine needles beneath one of the trees.

Ten yards away, the calm boy was lying on his belly. It interested Lee to see that he had removed his glasses, had laid them on the Greek book, and was now delving into a leather case the size of a tobacco pouch, which held certain odds and ends of cleaning equipment. Lee was further intrigued by the little vial of fluid that was about the size of a test tube, but with a cork in it. It served to make his glasses so transparent and bright. And now that his spectacles were in dazzling condition, would the boy finally shut his eyes and consent to sleep? Absolutely not. No, he had opened his text, had taken his pen—an old-fashioned appliance with a primitive-looking nib—and, with one eyebrow lifted in mild surprise, had begun to absorb some of the ancient language.

Lee possessed no such nib himself, and in any case, his eye was for the open corridor that seemed to run through the pines, the result, apparently, of a logging operation some years before. It led, in his imagination, to Calera and points even further than that. This much he did know, that once inside those trees, no adult could hope to find him. As for dogs, he had seen only one, a forlorn creature, old and tattered and weighed down with jowls. These were Lee's thoughts when, at that moment, the music master and his wife came riding up in a dilapidated truck.

Did they, perchance, come bringing gifts of food? No, the man had brought his guitar with him while the woman, her face flushed with excitement, began hurriedly unsheathing what appeared to be a flute. The very last Lee had expected was to be serenaded off to sleep by these two people. They played well, however. And their voices were sweet.

He woke at about half past 2 to find that the music master had departed and his role had been taken over by the above-mentioned white-haired geologist, who was still carrying the same basket of specimens over his arm. That Lee had slumbered through a great part of his presentation was obvious from the quantity of little, pale blue drawings the calm boy had set down in his notebook, including a cut-away view of the internal workings of a *seed*, Lee believed. Just now, the man was showing off a pine cone, turning the thing slowly in open view while at the same time pointing out with a pencil certain advantages of its rather elementary anatomy. He had much to say and many more things to show; Lee was not terribly surprised, therefore, to see him pluck from his collection a small living insect harnessed to a thread and pretend as if he might actually swallow it. No one laughed.

"This wicked wasp!" the man said. "But of course he's not any authentic wasp at all, no, but only a miserable little fly. However, I reckon if you strive to be another sort of creature, and do it over a long-enough period of time, why then" — his face lit up with pleasure — "you may actually turn out to be quite unlike what you were at the beginning! And that, of course, dear children, is why you're here."

Lee glanced at Philip, studying his expression. The bullet-headed boy, in the meantime, had gone off to the outer perimeter where he refused to have anything to do with the lecture or any of the specimens being handed around. Beyond, Lee could see the lake scintillating greenly in the afternoon and, on shore, a crowd of horses under the management of a man in a yellow shirt. The boys had turned sullen, and for a moment Lee began to believe that they might actually set upon the geologist and kill him, and then go running off through the woods before the hounds could be unleashed. Seeing their mood, the teacher stopped, blushed, grinned, mumbled a few more words about wasps and their things, and then began nervously returning the specimens to his basket.

"Yes!" Lee heard him say. "Nevertheless, it *was* an apt comparison all the same — wasps, boys. Well!"

They followed sullenly, saying nothing. Here between the mountains and the lake, the grounds had been measured out and broken down into any number of little quarter-acre gardens, some in flowers and some vines, and one given over entirely to yellow squash whose fruits had mostly been harvested by now. Lee saw what he considered to be the beginnings of an orchard, even if in his judgment the individual trees had been set much too close together. Further, he believed that he could identify five towering beehives, each a different color. They faced directly toward the east, as indeed they should. For it was only in this way that the insects might be awakened by the early sun and so get a proper start on each new day.

Geometry class was convoked in a trapezoidal structure built to wildly varying angles near the lake. Somewhat wary of it, Lee approached with care, his hands behind his back as he struggled to interpret the apothegm embossed in gilded letters just above the door. Fifteen centimeters tall, the words reiterated one of the more dubious truths of the first geometer of them all, a man previously known to Lee by name alone.

"Sit now," growled the professor, an emaciated person in a grey-and-black beard whom no one in his right mind would ever wish to irritate in any way. "And see to it that you maintain at least 60 degrees between your own persons and these other planes, but especially your chairs."

A groan went up from the boys. No longer did Lee consider the geologist the strangest person he had ever known. From his cloak, the man now withdrew a slide rule that was almost as long as a rifle, and then proceeded with unerring instinct to aim it at the four or five worst boys in the room. Lee then saw that he had other things on his podium which appeared to be toys in the form of wooden cubes, pies, pyramids and spheres.

"You have been allowed to enter this sacred place," he continued, "but shall not be allowed to leave it — not till each man of you has learnt his geometry."

There were groans. Lee pressed forward, determined to capture a personal copy from among the books the man had begun passing about. It contained, after he took one, all manner of diagrams in it mixed with text. Gathering up his best pencil, he waited for the lecture to begin. But instead:

"And why do you just sit there, each child of you staring back at me? Begin! Work! Learn! What? Protractors, you say? We have them in hundreds!" Indeed, the drawer was spilling over with them, as also with a number of other instruments that Lee could not immediately identify. "Nay, nay, sit apart from one another and let each child instruct himself. What? Need help, you say? Then let the strong instruct the weak! Provided, of course, that the weak be weak enough to ask for help."

And so they sat there like that, glancing from teacher to text and back again, and to the toys on top of desk. The bullet-headed boy, so good at swimming, appeared to be chewing sleepily upon a cud of some kind, and yet Lee could see the disquiet that had been growing in him as they moved further and further from mere bodily activities. This much Lee did know for certain, that he would have preferred to perish at once than seek help among persons of his own general size and type. Accordingly, he took up his book, a blue one with frayed corners but sound pages, and then drew off into the furthest corner of the room, where a giant-sized model of a protein molecule was moored to a pedestal.

He began the book from the first page. The light, it was true, was not terribly good here, and at first he had trouble remembering the names of all those whom the author had wished to thank. Next came dots and lines, and it was explained that the very nature of those things was violated by the need to represent them on paper. Your true line, as he understood it, was much more like where the page ended, ending suddenly and without so much as the slightest bit of ink to show where it theoretically went. More elusive still were the so-called *points*, so much shorter by far than even the briefest of lines. Lee, smoking, mulled this over, as well as the steel plate engraving of the world's first geometer, whose likeness was now, at last, revealed to Lee. Suddenly he glanced up to see that the calm boy, Philip, had inadvertently sat at the next table and seemed as displeased by Lee's proximity as Lee was by his. Young Burcham, dragging his book behind him, was going from boy to boy in search of aid.

Night came, bringing with it Lee's first authentic meal in as many days. Holding his knife and fork at the ready, he waited as the geologist sliced a good, thick portion of roast beef for him and covered it with gravy. The potatoes had been left whole and still had their skins on them. He approved of this, and also of the cooked apples sprinkled with cinnamon. He approved of the bread, too, a coarse stuff, very dark brown, in which the kernels had not always been ground down to perfect fineness. He also approved of the cider and took pride in its alcoholic content — the first time he had been offered any such thing. Focusing on the meat, he saw that it had a good grain to it and was about a quarter-inch or more in thickness.

There was to be no eating until Goldman had been served, and while they were waiting a thin and rather pale individual — Lee didn't much care for the looks of him — had arisen and was reading aloud in a tragic voice separated by many long pauses. Lee, by sight alone, had identified two sorts of beans on his platter, one of them slightly more appealing than the other. He liked to flavor them with molasses and lift them on his knife. Far across the room, Young Burcham had somehow landed among a group of the better students, where he sat eating fluently with a giant wooden spoon. The poetry then wandered off into a description of a famous banquet that had taken place in old times, a recitation that tended to make Lee's appetite still keener than it was. Philip! Lee saw how even this calmest and most serene of all young men, how even he, too, had taken off his glasses and put them wisely away to protect them from the heat and scents wafting from the meat and beans.

All this was as nothing, however, when compared to Goldman's methods. As enormous as he was, his bib a tablecloth and his head a monstrous-size quail's egg with the blunt end plunged into his neck, he ate with more fervor than any person there. Was it for that reason, or because his role required it, that he had a full table for himself alone? Or that he had been supplied with *two* women — Lee's table had but one — two of them running back and forth to keep his platter full?

Lee ate two baked apples in white cream and then, like Arnsdorf, the music professor, pushed back and lit up, not a pipe, but rather his fourth-to-last cigarette. The poetry had come to a close, the reader himself calling a halt to it just before succumbing to his emotions. The fire had burned down, but not before bequeathing a first-class bed of coals, half a foot thick. Staring into the glow, the scholars had fallen silent. Time passed as they waited for Goldman. Finally, at nine o'clock precisely, he came to his feet and stood blotting himself with his bib.

"We have completed our first day," he said.

They waited. Plainly, he was preparing to speak further.

"And tomorrow we'll do it again."

They still waited. Now came the real gravamen of this account, an exposition, highly digressive, that touched on just about everything:

"I can't promise," he said, "to foresee everything, but I do lay claim to this, namely, that we're moving into a time when we'll be so accustomed to invading small countries that we won't be able to stop. A time when our most famous people are also our worst, prisons are overflowing and great fortunes are being made on the backs of the naïve. The center is no good; therefore the center holds. Low culture drives out the high, and someday, not so far in the future, our last orchestra will have to dissolve itself for lack of funds. Boys! I foresee an army of mercenaries staffed mostly by women. After all, why should a man defend his country when he can hire someone else to do it? Television! We see what *that* has done. I tell you this, that if you cater to the average, the average devolves. We here, you and I, *we* aspire to the impossible, knowing that only one or two of us"—he pointed to Philip—"might get there someday."

He sat, but then immediately rose again on the arms of the two women who hurried to his support.

"Remember, boys, the eternal warfare between quality and its opposite. We *hate* equality, you and I, the most pernicious of all superstitions. No, I seem to see it now"—he closed his eyes and tapped at his forehead as if he had a headache—"the day when integrity will be considered a disgrace."

He went on. In his excitement, he had capsized his coffee, with much of it ending up in his lap.

"A good thing, education, but that's not mainly why we brought you here. No, advanced instinct is what we seek, refinement without end and the promotion of beauty over everything else. Did you know that the ordinary American man has completed his development before he reaches nineteen? That instead of love, boys and girls are hiring lawyers to negotiate coital contracts? What will it be fifty years from now—gentlemen walking about with their peters hanging out? Obesity redefined? Generals killing from long distances with ingenious machines? We may not have to wait until 2000 to see all that."

"Power flows to the center and doesn't come back again. Read the Constitution, boys, and learn to weep. The business of government is business, and the business of business is the business of taunting *us*. So how many Spartans will it take to destroy a system such as this? Ten thousand? Ten?"

One of the boys raised his hand, but Goldman ignored it.

"You're not going to be of any use, most of you—I can see that by looking at you. And yet, here and there, I see a face. That fellow over there, the one with the jawbone—*he* won't be afraid to get blood on his hands, yes?"

The fellow blushed. His jaw *was* prominent, and his eyes narrow and cold.

"Yes, we picked you out on purpose, my friend, and there's nothing you can do about it now!"

Four

Leland walked back slowly to the barracks, taking care not to lose himself in the dark. Some half-dozen boys had gathered in one of the rooms and, violating a primary rule, were conversing with one another. Standing off to one side, he listened with increasing skepticism to the boy named Wade, who had found a plank with a nail driven through it and was speaking—and much too airily, in Lee's opinion—of deeds of murder. Was he the man for it? To slaughter the director and run off through the woods? Lee thought not. Nor did he particularly wish to be drawn into this circle, the five or six of them who ran with the bullet-headed boy.

He was edging back toward his own chamber when he passed the partly-open door where Philip sat at his table, gazing down into his book of Greek. Apparently he had copied out a full page of the stuff, littering the sheet with that same pale blue ink that, seemingly, he stored in his fingers and in the magazines of his arm. Seeing all this, the neatness of the work, the blueness of the ink, the smartness of the boy… Lee shivered. For three seconds they glared at one another, until eventually the calm boy arose and came forward, and very courteously closed the door. Thus Lee found himself staring at a small, square card on which the boy had printed in pale blue ink the hours, and they were few, during which he was available for social activity.

In his own room, seated at his own table, Lee had neither ink nor pen to put it in. Instead, with the night getting darker and fog rolling in, he went to the window and dropped to the ground. The fields were empty, as was the orchard that lay between the library and the botanist's house. And that, of course, was when he remembered that he had left his fishing rod behind. It was difficult to reenter his room by way of the window and when he finally arrived there, he found Young Edmund seated on the cot.

"They're going to kill us! Kill, kill, kill us!"

"Oh, they are not neither. I already told you once!"

"Tell me again. Hey, I got an idea — why don't I just live here with you?"

Lee looked at him. The boy was a mess and had done so much crying that his eyes looked like asterisks, or like pennies with the engravings all washed away. Or rather, they looked like two far-off planets from which people used to wave to each other in better days.

"You can stay *one hour*, OK?"

It cheered him. Lee watched as, preparatory to climbing into bed, the boy emptied his pockets and lay the things in parallel formation on the desk. Most surprising was the money, ten and twenty dollar bills that had lost much of their coloration and appeared to have been left out for long periods in the rain. Even more surprising was the bone-handled knife, a handsome article of perhaps five inches in length with a mountain scene inscribed upon the blade. Looking more closely, Lee perceived what looked like a shepherd, a dog, and two sheep congregated just beneath the mountain's peak.

"Look at that knife!"

"I know."

They exulted over it. Lee had always loved precision tools, provided they were beautiful. Suddenly, the owner took it back and began to pretend that he was sawing with it against the arteries of his left wrist.

"See? I can kill myself *anytime I want*." He gave an evil grin.

Lee nodded. He had fed his fishing cane out through the window and was in a position, as soon as Burcham was asleep, to make his escape.

In actual fact, it took the better part of half an hour before the boy at last fell unconscious. Again, Lee prized open the window but had to wait until the moon agreed to run behind a cloud. Nothing could be seen, not until his eyes adjusted and he was able to make out the few wan lights that gave away the tutors' houses.

He raced forward, doing it crookedly lest he were being chased by bullets fired from across the lake. No dogs. In his exhilaration, and realizing that he was free — and confident, too, that no living soul could catch him once he reached the trees — he chortled as he ran. Could anything be more satisfactory than this? To baffle an entire community and tomorrow have his name on every tongue? Suddenly, he leapt, thinking to brush with his fingertips the black ceiling of the night that until now had been an inch or two out of reach.

But not tonight. Gloating, he entered the forest and continued on at a slower pace. How reverential it all was, these Alabama woods; even the fireflies signaled to each other with lanterns muted. No doubt about it, all things feared the night save only Lee, and night itself feared the coming of winter. But, until now, neither of them had admitted how late it actually was in the season, not until Lee blundered into a spider busily reeling in its ropes and tackle and packing them sadly away until next year.

He decided to travel with both hands held out in front of him — it was that dark. Certainly, his matches were of no use, nor his cigarette, and never mind how strenuously he sucked on it. Rather, it was the moon alone that he relied upon, together with a few significant stars.

It was near to midnight when he came to the crest of the ridge and began to analyze the two or three possible routes that might bring him home again. Below him, he could see a green and yellow brilliance composed of all the street lamps, cars, and neon signs that had coalesced so many years ago to form one, giant Birmingham profiled against the uninhabited counties that lay to the south-southwest. As for his own hometown — his mellow pillow, his candle and bed — he could not really hope to identify those from among so many other things, a café here and a filling station there, an office building over yonder and a residential section that continued to glow and pulse at 12:43 in the morning.

He had time. He was only thirteen and could well afford to wait until it was light. Accordingly, he found a place and then got down on his stomach and smoked. He could have slept, too, if he had chosen; instead, he now plucked from his vest the Greek language text gifted to him by the institution, but couldn't read in it until the moon came out.

It must have been past one in the morning before he again tried to pry open the book and review the list of ill-shaped characters out of which the ancients had been wont to fashion their writing. Already, the calm boy would have memorized each and every one of those signs, including even the most exaggerated of them. That was when the moon dipped once more behind the ridge. And if Lee was forced to wait upon it (and he was), nevertheless he could still be entertained by the sound of violin music sounding every few seconds in his head.

On his third attempt, holding the page just an inch in front of his nose, he learned the first letter, learned it thoroughly, and then stored it away in the closet of his mind where it had to abide in perfect loneliness for a while. Or until he sent others to join it.

Five

Having been promised horses, he awoke far too early the next morning and set off in high excitement toward the stables. Suddenly, disturbed by what he saw, he slowed and proceeded to move on tiptoes past the tremendous figure of Goldman sitting on shore in his armchair while gazing out, sadly, over the waves. He had a telescope in one hand and a very long fishing rod in the other that reached partway across the lake, neither of which he was using.

Either the man had not seen him or, if he had, had chosen not to speak. In any case, Lee quickly came to the dam itself and, gathering his courage, fled across it without toppling off onto the rocks a hundred feet below. He put no credence in the swans who, apparently, had spent the night in such close company with one another as to cause their sixteen necks to become hopelessly entwined. Of the trouts, he could see absolutely nothing, although he knew that they were there. It was because dawn had cast a sheen upon the lake, an opaque film as red as paint.

Knowing that he was being watched by the old man on shore, Lee tiptoed hurriedly toward the stables, where he was soon able to pick up the unmistakable snorting and stamping of animals who yearned to go for a morning run. In fact, they greeted him with an enthusiasm that he found almost embarrassing. Having searched in vain for oats or other feed, he went to the nearest of the stalls and knocked three times politely until the animal took the risk of putting its head through the opening. Lee was thirteen, this gelding somewhat younger; nevertheless, they looked at one another like affiliated souls. How soft its muzzle was! Softer than foam, albeit with numerous quills and bristles growing in it. Lee could not but see that the horse was somewhat disappointed, however. No doubt he had expected his meed of fodder, or a good-size cube of sugar at the least. Lee, who seldom went about with cubes of sugar in his possession, waited quietly while the creature went on sniffing with increasing dismay into his pockets and vest.

The next stall… Lee chose to avoid it, neither acknowledging nor being acknowledged by the rather sly-looking tenant who reminded him of someone he had known in the past. A mare came next, but not one that Lee would have wished to ride. She smiled and curtsied and, all in all, tended to debase herself, as if to inveigle from him the sugar that he didn't have. Instead, Lee proceeded to the following cell, where the sun's granulated beam, entering by way of a small, square, dust-covered window, fell precisely into the rather mirthful eye of an animal whose most urgent wish, like Lee's, was to go for a morning ride. Easily saddled, easily mounted and easily commanded, he could have driven this one all the way home.

Lee opened the portals and, with both of them trembling, led the horse out. By now the rampant sun had turned the lake from what had looked like paint to what now looked like gore. Coming down to shore, where Goldman could see them, Lee lit a cigarette and, putting on a rugged expression, sat looking off into the hills while his animal drank its fill of the stuff. That it was to be good weather today, good for horses and good for fishing and, yes, good for Greek as well, Lee knew from the way the lake suddenly turned transparent again, proving there were far many more trout in it than hiding places.

He had a good ride, quite exhilarating really, but found when he returned that breakfast was over and that the boys had gone to class. Continuing to the refectory, he knocked three times (politely) at the side door and waited for the Negress to open for him.

"I didn't get any breakfast," he explained.

"Sho nuff?"

They looked at each other.

"Can I have some?"

"No, you can't have none! You ain't got no business. Asides, they done et it all up!"

Lee reeled. "Well, could I have…"

She drew back in and shut the door, leaving Lee to wonder. Mounted as he was, he was almost as high as the roof beams. Higher still, he saw a flight of ducks moving south in broken formation. That was when the woman came, opened the door and, muttering, lifted out to him a square of burnt cornbread with a tad of butter on it.

The master's house had a trellis with dying roses, and it was to these that Lee tethered his mount. Having loosened the saddle cinch, he entered to find the boys reciting in unison, their heads bent low over their open books. Too late, he realized they were speaking in some other language and not the Greek that he had actually prepared. In the meantime the cornbread had largely turned to crumbs and he was reduced to licking them up one by one with his tongue. For one bad moment he thought the horse was about to stick his head through the window; instead, the carpenter, a whiskered man in an apron and bibbed trousers, came into the room and, after having determined which was Lee, handed over an envelope with a message in it. Lee accepted graciously and was about to put it away for future reference when he saw that the teacher, the carpenter, and boys were all waiting for him to read it.

Lee read it.

Having been summoned by the message, he entered the old-fashioned farmhouse where Goldman dwelt. The office itself was cluttered and small and apparently had served as a pantry at some time, to judge from the canned vegetables and jellies still sitting on the shelves. Lee noted the fishing tackle in the corner, the empty beer bottles, and the three little stand-up portraits of the man's defunct wife, a plain-looking sort of woman who hadn't wished to be photographed in the first place.

"Pig-headed, it says here."

"Yes, sir."

"Thinks well of himself. Is that how it is with you, Lee?"

Lee looked down.

"You need to understand something, my friend, we don't… What's the matter, you need to pee?"

"Not yet." He glanced at his watch.

"And another thing — who authorized you to go riding on my nag?"

"Nobody."

"Presumptuous, wasn't it? A little bit?"

"Yeah, but…"

"Quiet! Well, are you going to answer, or not?"

"Look, I never even wanted to come here in the first place! And besides, I…"

"O, I see. And so now you're going to throw *that* at us. I didn't think you'd do that son, I really didn't."

Lee looked down. The carpet was worn and old and had turned white where the sun had leached all the color away.

"And who authorized you to leave your room at 12:02 last night? No, these are the questions I'm confronted with. Every day, every day."

Lee lit a cigarette.

"You don't like the lake, is that what it is? Don't like my mare?"

"No, sir! I like 'em a lot!"

"Don't like the scholars I've assembled here for your benefit. You could have found better ones — it that it?"

"No, sir!"

They sat, examining each other in the gloom. Lee endured perhaps twenty seconds of it before transferring his gaze over to the photograph that sat on the shelf next to a jar of comb honey in which one of the original bees had been entombed. Finally, he looked at the bee itself — it was easier than meeting Goldman's gaze — a bee whose fate it was to tumble slowly and slowly, head over heels in the stuff forever.

"Food — he doesn't like the food."

"It's all right. I don't like them *beets* very much."

"Well, I'll tell you something, boy — if I was to come to *your* house, I don't believe I'd be as critical as you seem to be, no, sir. And I wouldn't be trying to run away all the time, neither. It's not a friendly thing to do, Lee, just isn't. No, I think if I was a guest like you, why, I think I'd just relax and try to enjoy it, know what I mean?"

"Yes, sir."

"Good! Well, then, we agree about that, I'm glad." He put forth his hand for shaking, a hand so grand that at first Lee tried to take only one finger, and not the largest, either. The third finger, he saw, had died, strangled to death in the grip of an antique wedding ring. "Good! And now, my friend, I need your advice. Tell me, what sort of penalty should I give someone like you?"

"I don't know."

"Someone who likes to ride on other peoples' horses."

"You could give me a warning, I guess."

Together they reflected on it. Lee realized that the servant was listening to it all, to reckon from how her shadow was continually passing back and forth in the hiatus beneath the door.

"Manure?"

"Sir?"

"You're a farm boy, aren't you?"

"Used to be."

"Well, there's our answer, then! You can spend the day shoveling manure."

Again they shook, although this time Lee avoided the atrophied finger. As for the servant, he would have said that she had atrophied long ago, having gelled, as it were, at the most indignant moment in her career. Nevertheless, Lee went on smiling at her, which is to say until he ruined everything by turning and bowing to her in his exaggerated way.

He was ushered to the barn by the horse wrangler, a bitter-looking quantity who preferred to squint off into the mountains than to look anyone in the face. It was apparent that he vehemently resented being distracted from his. Lee was sympathetic, as he had not yet been in this place for three full days and still hadn't accomplished any fishing whatsoever — these were his thoughts when, suddenly, he halted and jumped back, astonished to see that the calm boy had arrived there before him and was working in the manure. And what, Lee asked himself, had been *his* particular crime?

They set to work. Of the wheelbarrows, Philip's was better. On the other hand, or rather other hands, Lee's hands were undoubtedly the more experienced. Of the shovels, Lee would have preferred the other boy's, which appeared so much more serviceable than his own. Of manure, there was enough for both of them.

Of glasses, Lee already saw a smudge on Philip's left lens, a development that cheered him out of all proportion and caused him to believe that, with his own unobstructed vision, he could out-labor the boy with one hand while reserving the other for his smoking habit. He soon saw his mistake, however. Glasses or not, there was nothing wrong with either the boy's energy or his dedication to the project that lay all around them. Lee was disappointed to see how quickly he had acquired the art of it, never overfilling the barrow, nor yet underfilling it, causing unnecessary trips to the garden. Of unnecessary trips, Lee made several. *His* barrow was cranky and had an out-of-kilter tire that wanted to go off in its own direction. Watching them compete with each other, the wrangler's mood had brightened, his usual morose nature turning to outright chuckles as he turned and strode off down the hill. That was when Lee caught sight of the twenty-six boys pilgrimaging off to their next lesson, among them Young Edmund Burcham, who appeared not to be crying. He continued to keep his hand in his pocket, however, where he could stay within quick reach of his suicide knife.

Philip and Lee wouldn't look at each other. The calm boy had learned to drive his barrow headlong into the heap and allow it to fill itself, as it were, before then jogging off to the garden where the stuff was to be applied. Lee was in some real danger of being outdone by him, a city boy dressed in glasses; instead, at that moment, he stumbled forward suddenly and landed up to his elbows in the stuff. Lee was extremely pleased. Those bright glasses, formerly the best part of him, were mostly opaque now.

Later, looking back upon it, Lee could not honestly say which of them had moved the greater amount of manure. Having done with it, they stacked their shovels and then, still not speaking to one another, padded on down to the lakeside in order to bathe. By far the better swimmer, Lee immediately took off his clothes and went to deep water and splashed about in it. The mean temperature, he believed, was somewhere between seventy and eighty degrees of mercury, and he wanted to take advantage of it as much as possible before winter came. Could anything be stranger than ordinary water? It fell apart in front of him, and when he tried to lift a portion of it in his hand, its complexion changed from blue to transparent. Suddenly, he veered off and began to follow a trout running at high speed for the depths.

Nothing could have surprised him more than to find young Philip sitting in great calmness on the bottom, his two milk-white lenses scintillating in the murk. The boy was a better swimmer than Lee had thought. Here, Lee stopped and waited, assuming that the boy would soon wish to climb back to the surface. But after another half-minute had gone by, and he still remained sitting there with folded arms...

Lee came and sat across from him. Better to die, he believed, or drown, than to be bettered by such a person as this. He knew, of course, that after a certain time without oxygen, the human brain begins to rot. Accordingly, he tried to think of other things, until these thoughts, too, turned to oxygen and air. Meanwhile, Philip had taken off those sparkling glasses of his and, with his expression more serene than usual, even for him, was pretending to polish one of the lenses between his thumb and finger.

Later, Lee recollected that his brain had not, after all, begun to rot, not until two full minutes or more had gone by, awful ones growing continually more awful, right up until the other boy put his glasses on and gazed longingly upwards toward the oxygen and the air.

Six

A well-attested type, Arnsdorf, the Master of Music, Rhetoric, and Tennis, was an irritable man, atrabilious in the morning and choleric at night. They stood face-to-face, each man looking the other up and down in the vestibule of the enormous home with its books and prints and goldfish and — and this gave Lee particular pleasure — its "T"-shaped dining table loaded with food. Suddenly, the man yanked off his glasses and, bending near, began to examine Lee's facial arrangement and bony structure. Lee was a simple-looking youth, and his ears stuck out.

"Ah, Lord," the professor said. "However, I never allow myself to form final judgments this early in the semester."

Lee thanked him.

"But tell me, were you at all disturbed last night? Owing, possibly, to a certain violin concerto going off every half-hour in your ear?"

Lee thought about it. It did seem to him that something of that sort had taken place.

"Hee! Hee, hee. And now you'll never be the same! Want to hear another one?"

"I reckon not."

"He doesn't want any more!" He roared with delight, even going into a brief but very evil little dance, unpleasant to watch. He was the oddest man yet and, owing to his warts, one of the ugliest in the valley. Lee might be able to count fifty hairs upon his head, each of them combed out to full length and held in place with staples. "And yet," he went on, "someday you'll be running to this little cottage of mine to beg for crumbs. *Musical* crumbs, I mean, not literal ones."

Lee doubted it. Primarily he was looking at the man's wife, a merry sort of woman, not without warts of her own, who had been condemned to go through life with a jolly little secret that kept her smiling non-stop. Just now, she was scampering back and forth to the kitchen with an excitement that broke through from moment to moment in the form of giggles and snorts.

"Ignore her," the man said, "if you can. One gets used to it after a certain while. She *is* a good cook, however."

They came to the table from a long distance, approaching with long steps from widely separated quadrants of the room. Lee's nose was for the sweet potatoes which appeared to have a glaze on them, possibly of brown sugar. But his eye, *that* was for the duckling and the trout.

"Goldman's concept," the man went on, speaking hurriedly as he attached a bib about his neck and smoothed it down. "Inviting you fellows into our actual living quarters. Me, I hold with Sigmund — that my home is holy to me."

Lee, reaching for the biscuits, had to agree.

"Ah, yes, old Leland Pefley, so. Couldn't help but notice how you chose to avoid my class this morning. Interesting. And no doubt that will be your way of showing that you don't approve of my teaching methods?"

"No, sir! I just.."

"Yes?"

"Had to shovel manure."

"Manure. You're speaking of Spivey's class, of course."

"No, sir; *real* manure."

"Ho. Sounds like one of Goldman's stunts. He must have been very, very peeved with you, Leland. What did you do?"

"Aw, I just rode his ole horse, that's all. Heck, I didn't even know it was his!" The potatoes were good.

"You rode on Beauregard?"

"Just a little bit."

"Oh my stars, the child rode on Beauregard! That's not done, Lee, it just isn't!"

"I just went up to Hogwallow Point and back." Melted marshmallows covered the potatoes to various depths.

"Rode Beauregard! And then he was made to shovel... Have you bathed?"

"Yeah, but Philip, he was made to, too."

"Ah, Philip. Now there is *one gifted young man*. He can miss one of my classes and get away with it. But not you, Lee; not you."

The potatoes had been wrought into a compote, and this in turn was covered not with just a marshmallow glaze alone. It was also glazed in honey. Lee went for it, his hand, at the last moment, stumbling up against a platter of smiling lake trout lying side by side within a dense white sauce.

"Eat up!" the man said. "First we chow, and then music thereafter — isn't that how it's supposed to be? Eat, eat!"

Lee did. His hosts were particularly good at this, and the woman even more so than the man. It disconcerted him to see how she dipped so daintily into the sauce and then, beckoning to the largest of the trout, how she seized upon it, smiling sweetly as she snapped its spine. But soon his fascination turned to outright amazement when he saw how she dealt with bones. Never had the boy seen so much power in a woman's jaw, nor teeth like hers, whose function, design, and true purpose were as evident as a hippopotamus's.

"What, you don't like the pork?"

"I'm going as fast as I can!"

"Makes me mad — I take it as an insult — people who don't know what's good."

"Yeah, but…!"

"Eat, eat!"

They pushed back at last and then drew off into widely-separated chairs where the woman right away fell into a stupor of some kind. Behind them, Lee caught a last glimpse of the table itself with its bones and trash, its cantaloupe rinds, spilt wine, and some dozen denuded corn cobs whose kernels appeared to have been surgically removed. The professor now wore an expression as glazed as the potatoes and as sleepy as the woman's. Lee thought at first he might actually tumble off onto the floor; instead, two minutes having gone by in relative silence, he spoke:

"So."

"Yes, sir; it was good. *Real* good!"

"Well, of course it was good. It's always good, when *she's* at the helm."

"Yes, sir."

"But don't imagine that we're finished, certainly not."

"We're not?"

"By no means! However, this time we'll have Haydn with the sausage and Bartók with the pie."

It was late in the evening and getting later when Lee finally pushed back for the second time, nor would he ever wish to eat again. Sleepily, he gazed down the length of the room, his perspective coming to a sudden halt when it ran up against the man's impressive hoard of books.

"Yes, my books — I can see that you are looking at them. Very well, come forward now, child, and I'll introduce them to you. And you to them."

He would have preferred to sleep; nevertheless, he rose up unsteadily and approached obliquely from the leeward side. The room was long and the man stood waiting with increasing impatience for his arrival. Finally:

"Yes, here you are, good. Now, it's true that I've done a fair amount of... Would you *kindly* put that cigarette out? Imagine!"

Lee put it out.

"Fair amount of reading in this room. Yes, and great suffering, too. It's a terrible business, Pefley, to maintain one's books in such tight propinquity with one's music. The stress. You see that great, fat volume up yonder on the top shelf? The blue one?"

"Yes, sir."

"And now you know why *I'm* so fat. Put your finger on it. No, no, not on *me*! *Dieu*!"

Lee took his finger back and put it on the book. He had to stand on tiptoes so that his eye, if not indeed his nose, was forced to look upon, if not indeed to whiff, a pale yellow volume with myriads of bookmarks protruding above the pages.

"And does it not 'tingle beneath thine touch,' as Hooker says? Better yet than sweet potatoes? E'en with their glaze?" Suddenly, blushing deeply, the man turned and addressed himself to his wife, who seemed mostly asleep, as Lee believed. "Not that the potatoes were anything but excellent. Very much so, yes indeed, quite marvelous, really."

Lee looked from him to her and back again. This pair, added up together, were even stranger than Goldman in combination with the photographs of his extinguished wife. As for these books (and he was getting tired of standing on tiptoes), some were slim and some were green, and some came in languages that he could not immediately name.

"Remember, Pefley, that you have been badly deceived about life and education. We did not, repeat *not*, fetch you here for the usual secular reasons. 'Preparation for life, etcetera, etcetera. Job training. Democratic participation. No! *Our* purpose is to quash life and go beyond it, and end up on the other side. But are you listening?"

"Yes, sir. Quash."

"And go beyond it."

"Way beyond."

"But are you listening? Remember, Lee, that life, 'life in the round,' life of the ordinary kind, is for the little man, the realm of getting a living, of doings and of things, *maya's* web. Your assignment is to participate in all that as little as may be necessary and… You smile?"

Lee was not smiling.

"… as may be necessary."

Lee nodded. Far away, he could hear desultory barking, his first serious indication that the academy might, in truth, be reinforced with dogs.

"But are you listening? Remember, Lee, remember economics, policy, and even war itself are but the preoccupations of people who have nothing in them and who must therefore constantly be thrashing about and meddling in the world."

"And *my* job…"

"Policy, prices, agriculture and internal combustion machines. Oh, I don't say we can ignore them *utterly*."

"Heck, no."

"What?"

"Can't ignore 'em *utterly*."

"And here's the proof, Lee, that all those who have tasted, however remotely, of man's real business, the business sometimes called beauty and sometimes other things… Well! They'll opt for that every time!"

"Well, shoot, yeah."

"But are you listening? Remember, Lee, that beauty itself would still exist even if humans had never arisen."

The boy nodded dubiously, never imagining that he would someday come to believe the same.

"But are you the man for it, and are you listening? To eschew the little people and maximize the time that you are not in their presence? Remember! The smaller the man, the more he will be concerned with the people's weal. But the grander the man… Oh! Your grand man doesn't care a fig what happens to people."

Lee raised his hand to speak. The man pushed it down again.

"Weal, my ass! The truth is, Lee, we have good reason to believe that the people ought not have very much weal. Bad for poetry. And I *know* what it has done to music."

"Yes, sir. Me now, I…"

"Eschew them! Eschew them all, betas and gammas and public men, eschew it all if you hope to slither through the wealth-and-position web."

Lee agreed to it, and then returned with the man to the table where they ate more pie while spitting up numbers of cherry seeds that bounced off the platters. It was clear to Lee that the man did some of his most stormy thinking here along with his meals. And as if that were not enough, the woman had topped off each individual wedge of pie with a five-dram flitch of yellow cheese that had been flecked, fore and aft, with a cinnamon powder that almost resembled rust. Very little did Lee see of that rust, owing to the ice cream that covered it. Finally, they pushed back for the third time but declined to leave their chairs until the Bartók had come to an end. All during the music and the pie, the man's mood had been improving; now, sipping at the wine — and this represented only the second wine that Lee had ever tasted — he spoke out loud and clear:

"Hold! Give over! Yes, yes, put on the Melchior, dear, and let us see how far the boy, having done so well at table, how far he… But think of it like this, Leeward, that music is but a 'searchlight' by aid of which we may sometimes, if but briefly, descry that 'further shore' that is the authentic goal of education, properly so-called."

Lee wished to show how much he agreed with that, but could not effectively do so with the room as flooded as it was in opera music. It was only music, and not of Lee's favorite type, either. And then, too, it appeared odd to him that the man would choose to go on raving in the midst of sounds that he putatively adored.

"I ask you, Lee, can you imagine a man like that" — he pointed with his wine glass toward one of the portraits on the wall — "a man like that dawdling around a voting booth? No, no, that's the *infinite* you hear there, the divine, even if you haven't the slightest notion of what I'm talking about."

"No, sir."

"Good, good. The best five minutes in history, and you about to go to sleep. Ah, well." And then: "But, yes, the pie *was* good, however." And then finally: "Just ignore her, if you can." Because she was smiling and snoring at the same time.

Seven

He ran back to his room in the dark. As utterly and as absolutely exhausted as he was, his spiritual condition was nevertheless good. A hundred lamps were flickering from various points in the valley, each representing a student at his desk, a master preparing the next day's lesson, or signifying an effort to ward away the bears who came at night to open the hives and probe for trout.

Lee hurried. The levee appeared to be higher than it was, and when he finally came to the top of it and saw the river, a blue-green unguent similar to electricity, and saw three armadillos emerge from the woods in single file and then go shunting off across the dam in order of size, when he saw all this and several other things as well, such as the clouds that had been remanded to the western sky… Well! That was when he uttered out loud in increasing amazement at this place, unable to say whether it was simple bitterness he felt, or whether, in his case, even that was outweighed by still further amazement.

The ridge of mountains hesitated in mid-air, still declining to collapse upon them and wash away the South. Coming to the lakeside, he marveled at how this body of water fit so seamlessly into its sixteen-acre bed. Better still was the "furnace," as he called it, that sat in the depths of the lake and pulsed and gleamed and waned, and sometimes went out altogether. And so might not this be the best of times to flee from here — now, while the hounds were groggy? No. Instead, he tightened the strap that held his books together and then, taking a cigarette, ran down along the dark side of the levee.

Generally, it was his custom to select his dreams in advance and, while getting into his pajamas, to sketch out the script and denouement and make last-minute adjustments in the plot. Tonight, he had resolved to put aside that old love affair of four years ago and imagine himself on board a seafaring vessel of the galleon class, a stately one under full sail with maps unscrolled on the captain's table and a single lantern glowing yellowly across a Sixteenth-century ocean — it was one of his primary and most reliable dreams. Suddenly, he reminded himself that he had an assignment, the heaviest that had ever been inflicted upon him, to read a full forty pages in a certain blue, boring book that itself weighed near to forty pounds.

Lee cursed, his gorgeous dream gliding away on the tide. And when he finally agreed to take down the book and arrange it in the precise center — he was fastidious in these matters — precise center of his antique and rather discolored desk, and agreed to open it... He jumped back, greatly surprised to see that the margins were running over with commentary set down in a penmanship so microscopic that he saw at once how percipient had been the man who did it, and how boring, too. For he knew well how, in the adult world, those two attributes always went hand-in-hand.

Fortunately for the future of his development, the book also had a woodblock frontispiece engraving plate picturing a raven winging bravely toward the sun. *Un*fortunately, the bird was transporting a large serpent in its claws, which was preparing to strike. Lee studied it, uncertain how the snake could dare to use its fangs without also incurring a very bad fall all the way to the ground. Mulling on this and other things, he rose and strode about the room.

In fact, the book had more than just one engraving in it, but Lee did not feel entitled to spy upon them until he had read the intervening pages. Soon he began to enjoy the glosses more than the text, especially in those places where the commentator had added little drawings that, however, began to deteriorate into mere doodling once he got past page nineteen. Suddenly, Lee jumped back again, stymied at the point where the man had shifted over into what looked like Latin. He had no recourse but to go back to the narration, which was in English, and start at the beginning.

Lee might have been more tolerant of books, if only he had been able to take up the full substance of them in one fell moment, while evading the very tedious reading process which tended to eat up so much time. And then, too, he had not completely abandoned his sea-going dream.

An hour having gone past slowly, Lee stood up again. From his position, he could see the fire warden's tower in the hills where, at just this moment, the man himself was sitting at his window. His desk had a lamp or candle on it, the same flickering candle or lamp that had already enticed Lee off to sleep a thousand times at home, albeit from a wildly unlike angle. Trigonometrically speaking, he believed that he must be a good twenty miles or more from home, a considerable sprint, much too far to undertake before the dawn.

For two hours, he went on reading until, around three in the morning, he began to gag upon the wisdom accumulating in his head. The other book, the one with the torn cover, was smaller, shorter, freer of glosses, and more to the point had a cheerful jacket on it that pictured a youth extraordinarily like himself. Lee came nearer, nodding as, one by one, he recognized the boy's good intentions, the sincerity in his face, and the rest of those traits. Now, setting it up precisely in the center of his desk, he forced the book open against weak resistance and began to read. In reading, he soon began to feel that many of the dead were reading over his shoulder with him — such were the hallucinations one had at 3:46 in the morning. Suddenly, while he nodded off, a planet burst asunder in the upper window, lingered for a moment, and then again blazed up very brightly before dying amid a hail of sparks. Lee leapt from the desk and retreated into a corner of his room, only distantly conscious of the screams and exclamations coming from the other cells. From his high position, the fire warden was apparently giving very little attention to it. He simply could not afford to perturb himself over each and every little starburst or sundry explosion in the night, not unless he wished to go completely insane. Lee glanced at the pond with its furnace and green chambers, finding there a magnified reflection of the warden tippling in his office, too drunk and too blasé to care about what might happen in the sky.

It was late, the child was tired, and he had scarcely two hours in which to bank a bit of sleep before morning came; nevertheless, he now arose for the third time and took down the heaviest of the books, lifting it in both arms and then positioning it in such a way so that it overlapped both edges of the desk to an equal degree. But this time the margins, which in any case had been over-pruned by the binder's knife, held only very inferior sorts of notes in them, including, in one place, a grocery list. Lee read three pages in succession, murky stuff that referred back constantly to a fold-out map showing where a world-famous slaughter had taken place in old times. This was most odd — there was not a spot anywhere on that map that he could touch with his pencil point without at the same time hitting upon a place where someone had died or suffered or performed a murder. And now, all of that had been reduced to mere gossip drawn in fading ink upon poor-grade paper. (He was only thirteen, and had had no association as yet with those "aesthetic experiences" that were to figure so importantly in his future.) And that was when a thought struck him — that of all the people in this maddest of all communities, that he alone was awake just now, still conscious, still smoking and still reading, still hearing screams and violins.

Eight

At the time of the bringing in of the corn, seven weeks had gone by. But now, instead of the original twenty-six, there were but nineteen boys to accomplish the work, all the others having been loaded aboard the bus and transported back to whence they had come. Lee felt no grief at seeing them go. On the contrary! He could have cited at least another dozen whom he would have liked to send back, not just to Birmingham and Atlanta indeed, but to points even further than that.

He was humming as he worked. It was an adequate day — full sun, the air washed clean by a recent rain — and the corn was high and sufficiently ripe. Consequently, he had to stand on tiptoes if he wished to collect the topmost ears that, as often as not, had already been visited by the ravens and crows. But even if the cobs had but one remaining kernel, or none, Lee still tossed all of them into the wagon in obedience to Goldman's decree. And was he counting the cobs, that man, as he sat in his elevated place beneath a beach umbrella to fend off the October sun? This man understood nothing of crops and the life of farmers, and yet there was not one gardener, scholar, bricklayer, nor scullery maid willing to say it to his face. Twice, Lee had seen Arnsdorf himself make an approach to the man, only to lose heart and veer off at the last moment in some other direction.

They labored on until just after ten, at which time Edmund came racing up, almost too late to share in the work. It is true that his little basket held only three cobs, requiring him to make innumerable short trips to the lorry where a winter's worth of corn already lay in exemplary rows that hinted at Lee's strong influence upon the operation. And, if still there was dew upon the stalks (and there was), and if the leaves were still brittle (they were) and came to sharp points, it didn't matter, since Lee and Philip and several others had come dressed in gloves for just that reason.

By noon they had brought in such a quantity of the stuff ("Hesiod's gold," as the Greek professor enjoyed calling it) that several of them were ready to quit. Not Lee, who continued his search for the superior cobs, plenteous ones full of grain, each fitted out in a perfectly-adapted suit of shucks as crisp as manuscript. Had he been reading too much? Very probably so, to judge by how his head kept reverting to certain poets who had been forced upon him against his will. Sidling up to the wagon, he tried to foist some of those memorable lines off onto the mule, an alert animal with steeple-like ears who was slowly becoming hardened to it, ruined by lyrics.

It was near to noon when the harvesters paused long enough to watch a crowd of dullard boys, some five or six of them, being driven to the outer fields by the orchard manager, a hard man who took pleasure in his work. Lee was particularly gratified to find the bullet-headed boy among them, but less pleased to see that the tiny Burt had also been inserted into this group. Lee signaled to him, realizing too late that the boy could not wave back, not unless he wished to drop his hoe and mallet and the rather primitive-looking adze he was dragging. That was when the book steward, a man called "Spivey," the poorest corn-picker in the valley, came up to Lee and stood beside him.

"Bringing in the corn! Lord, I do hate it so."

"Do it *this* way," Lee said. "Make it do what *you* want it to do, instead of what *it* wants."

"Yes!"

"Just break 'em off. It don't hurt 'em."

"Yes! Now I see the shrewdness of it. Devilish business. No, you'll go far."

Lee followed, monitoring the man's technique. He was still not terribly good at it. He moved too hesitantly over the broken ground and was wrongly dressed, having reported for work in his robe and slippers and a scarf of some kind. His hair and complexion were grey, both of which sorted extremely well with the powder-blue kerchief tucked into his sleeve. Moving in tandem down the row, Lee was surprised to hear him say:

"You visit other people. You never visit me."

"Yeah, but..."

"*I* have knowledge."

"Sure, but..."

"And books, oh! More than Arnsdorf, who uses his spare space for food and eatables. All right, he has books, I admit it. But not like mine, Lee. Not like mine."

"I reckon I could come..."

"Yes?"

"...tomorrow."

"Tomorrow! And none too soon, either, not if you want to free yourself of... How shall I say? Red clay ignorance that clings to your face?"

"Aw, shoot. Look, I'm getting real tired of..."

"But are we here to talk? Or gather maize? I think we must decide, no?"

"Maize," Lee said, enunciating it gloomily. He no longer followed after the man. And then, too, Goldman was awake, Edmund whistling, mule listening, and the corn putting up a last resistance as time itself was wasting.

Nine

After waiting until November, Lee departed from his room. Soon frost would be making an appearance, it was darker than usual, he was carrying two books, and smoke was rising from the hills. Noiselessly, he crept to Philip's window, and, after wiping the condensation off a spot of about two square inches, stood spying upon the boy who had been laboring for the past week amid a clutter of drawings and one huge microscope, probably now attached forever to his sky-colored eye. The varlet had continued to organize his books by theme instead of size, an all-too-pragmatic way of doing things that tended to make Lee's gorge rise. They stared at each other through the window.

The night was turbid. Running past on tiptoes, Lee hurried down to the lake, now appearing as if on fire, and began to ascend the first of the low-lying hills that characterized the view on that side. He could not honestly recall having ever seen the moon in such a sorry state, in rags and tatters as it were, and so altogether at the mercy of the ravens now pecking remorselessly at it. His mind flew back to his youth and to the shock that had come over him upon being told that the sun and moon were not, and never had been, one identical orb in two different modes. Or that the American states, which he had memorized alphabetically, were by no means arranged on the map that way. Or that dogs and cats were not, in fact, the male and female of one single order. Forced to choose, Lee, of course, had opted for moon, dogs, Alabama, and all other bale-boding things in general.

It was a short sprint to the next ridge where the fog, though tenuous, was still dense enough to keep him from reading. It was an old district, geologically speaking, already ancient when the on-rushing Cenozoic had elbowed its way into the valley, bringing with it that nauseating broth of lava in which so many fossils had congealed. *Astronomically* considered, all this was nothing, of course, quite trivial really, a simple nuisance when compared to transactions on the stars. But now Lee's mind turned away even from the stars, choosing rather to think on *metaphysical* time, the product of his readings, and in comparison to which all these stars and rocks and whatnot constituted but one blink in the eye of that Nilotic toad-god levitating on his lily pad. And when Lee focused upon the long succession of toads, those thousand thousand generations, each blink an eon and every world an egg… Well! That was when he got down in the grass and lay for a time on his belly.

It was near to midnight before he came into the true hills, so much higher by far than where he had napped. Here, he was within those regions of fume and mist that might make it seem to anyone watching from a distance that the hills would go on smoldering forever, or until Time itself called for a stop. He could pluck individual atoms out of the fog and hold them between thumb and finger until they resolved to water, leaving him with nothing to do but throw them away. The pines, horribly shaped, were full of eyes. Already he had climbed too high to be taken back to the institution without his own cooperation. Nor did he still suffer from fear of the hounds, given their known intolerance for elevations such as these.

Far below and well off in the distance, he could see the miniature Birmingham clustered for warmth around two giant furnaces spitting out gleeds that rose and fell, sometimes setting homes on fire. He saw more; changing positions, he saw what appeared to be a sandstone colossus representing the seated figure of the philosopher whom Lee had recently been reading. And if the man was eroded about the face and listed to one side, yet was he also staring continually in wide-eyed horror at truths too awful for most colossi to abide.

He did try to read once more, but found the moon too undependable. And when he gazed across at the next peak, he could not be absolutely certain there was not another little boy over there with a book of his own. Lee signaled to him and then, getting no reply, began bringing together the materials for a fire.

Only two matches still remained to him; fortunately, he was good at husbanding such things. And if he had lately been reading of how great Tamerlane once had built a heap of 50,000 heads, Lee must be content with pine cones, fifty of them. Both matches were needed, and even then he had to fan at it with his vest before it burst into full flame. He gloated and danced and then, having warmed his book and hands, turned and bowed sweepingly in the direction of the tower while hoping that he and his work might be seen in the binoculars of the star warden, an ignorant man who kept the hills.

He wanted to burn the mountain and the earth along with it; instead, he relented at the last minute and kicked the fire to pieces and pissed on it. This was nothing. Someday he would do things, such things, such very dread things as to send God Himself into shock. And if any should catch him at it (doing things), why, then, let him deserve to be caught — such was his philosophy, then *and* later.

It was past one in the morning when he came to the highest point in the whole Croatoan range and, shielding his eyes, brought into focus one grey ridge after another riding off to infinity. There, where the mountains appeared to have broken down under the impact of time, there in that direction lay the sea. But first came Georgia and the pine lands that had comprised some of the choicest parts of the whole Confederacy. Now, at last he was able to read, a process made easier by the increase of starlight at this elevation.

He gave his attention to one star in particular, a "lilac dwarf," as science called it. Bloated to immense size and radical brightness, it covered the place where the constellation Vega used to dwell. Availing himself of it, Lee skipped forward in the book, finishing two full pages before the light began to shudder and, finally, shut down altogether when a crowd of horse-shaped clouds came galloping up. But Lee, who sometimes liked to imagine that he was riding on the debris of exploded stars, found new sources of light in Sagittarius. And did he see harbingers in this of that new epoch in educational theory that was always portending down in the valley? No. No, it was only bright light, nothing else.

Lee reached for a cigarette (but didn't find one), and then brought his watch up near to his strongest eye and spent some time gazing in at the black-faced dial that overlapped the sky. It was his best moment in the best hour of the night, when Alabama's prevailing evil, the sin called "activity," was at the apex of its nadir.

At 5:15, the moon was down, the sun threatening, clouds far apart, and dawn turning out to be a disaster scattering fireflies from their routes. And so it was with Lee; miles from the Academy, he found himself at 5:27 looking down into his father's farmyard where he expected, at any moment, to see himself, or one just like him, going through his morning crafts with good intentions, harkening to the horses and hieing to the mules. Ought not Lee to at least go in among the hens and say his say? A last farewell to comfort them, through the remnant of their very bad fates? He had only to drop down the hill, take the key from its location, and be a boy again; instead, he turned and went back up the path a distance. It was a long jaunt he faced, and in places it was precipitous. However — and in this he somewhat resembled one of his professors — he had become skilled at reading on the trail.

Ten

The village was old, older than old, with grants and patents running back to Charlemagne's time. The levee, too, was old, which Lee now stepped forward from the forest to salute. Strangely, the sun had only partially risen today — it was a Wednesday — and appeared to be resting on the levee itself. Shielding his eyes, Lee observed a Negress, a tall one in a bright bandanna, moving across the horizon with a decanter of milk balanced on her head. Also a little girl running along behind whose own decanter was probably empty by now, to judge by how she hopped and skipped and bounced along the trail. Lee dodged this way and that, struggling to get out from behind his cigarette smoke in time to see the woman and child *step into the sun itself*, as if they thought to quench with rations of milk as small as theirs a thirst as huge as its. Tragically, he saw only one of them come out again, and then go bouncing gaily down the path.

Keeping out from under the sun, Lee now scrambled to the ridge of the levee where by hap he immediately fell in with a large family of black people — it was Sunday, not Wednesday; Lee was very often wrong about these things -padding off to church in order of age and size. Below him, the whole landscape had been rendered mauve and yellow by reason of so many squashes and pumpkins lying at hazard. Apples, too, great numbers of them decaying forgottenly on the stem. The pigs disdained the apples but not the squash, and seemed to be turning into hogs even as he gazed upon them. Alabama was definitely going to seed, and every leaf was in a flutter to show off its nether side. He chose not to speak of it however, nor talk to himself (his most recent bad habit), nor take out his book and read, not so long as he was following along in the midst of a family who were slowing down, or going faster, or stopping altogether in a continuing effort to be free of him.

He smoked. It was chilly for this time of year and he believed that he could count several dozen spumes of smoke lifting from a similar number of shacks (each shack with its cow) that sat off well apart from each other in the valley. He knew, of course, how hard winter was upon the poor. And hard upon the hounds—he saw one now, a rueful creature whose paper-thin ears fell down on both sides and left a trail of runnels in the sand. The dogs of Negroes! It was almost never mentioned how quickly and how prone such dogs were to turning into Negroes, too. This one had crawled up under his master's cabin and seemed inclined to remain there in bitterness, or 'til Lee and winter agreed to go away.

Lee went away. In the distance he could see evidence of forethought on the part of the city's founders—that no matter how tall the trees might grow to be, the church and steeple would still be higher by an inch or two at least. It served as a pylon for the bats and swallows who loved to wheel about it in the course of that make-believe war these two species had been carrying on. But as to the people, what, pray, might *they* be doing within those tattered shacks? And when December came? And those yet darker months that followed in December's wake? Who, then, would stop the weather from entering through windows covered only in burlap and brown paper? He saw one home, indeed, that had washed up so near to the levee that a small brown goat had actually stepped off onto its turfen roof and was grazing there. Here, too, a kite had become entangled in the branches of a pine. And although the child himself had no doubt grown up by now and gone away, had lived and died, the kite itself was fluttering still.

The town was silent. He encountered a mill worker covered in flour and then a wagon laden down with a whole nation of hens, each in a tiny cage of her own. Lee mistrusted these drivers, knowing well their reputation for spitting black juices down upon boys, dogs, mules and, sometimes, other drivers. (They seldom spit upon white women and girls, however.) The danger having passed, he was able to turn his attention to the six noble-looking widows who sat facing one another from the porches of the town's five noblest homes. He waved to each of them in turn, receiving various sorts of responses. But as to that noblest of them all, a frail woman in laces and broaches who preferred to remain indoors and reconnoiter through the curtains... Here, Lee halted, turned, and then bowed sweepingly with accompanying flourishes.

He continued direct to the grocer's and bought a full carton of cigarettes from a worried-looking man in an apron who seemed disinclined to hand them over. The place was like a pharmacy, with row after row of well-organized bottles and jars with labels on them — reading material in great plenty. He particularly noticed a hoard of sardines that, to read what was written on the cans, derived from the Lithuanian Sea. And in short, he delighted in complex arrangements of well-labeled things. He scanned up and down a shelf of bottled olives, some of them putrefying within a medium that had broken down into acids with mold floating on top. Had he been reading too much? He was also uneasy about the three old men, morose types sitting about the stove wearing extinct expressions. The last he wanted at this time was to be made to stand and listen to the witticisms that they soon would be throwing in his direction, a usage so much the worse, by far, to his thinking than being spat upon by cotton haulers. And yet these could have been great people, every one, but at some point had opted to be ordinary instead. (It's easier that way.) Looking at them, Lee concluded that if this was the best that life had to offer, it was better never to have lived at all. "Who won the game?" he was tempted to ask, and "what kind of gas mileage you getting these days?"

The book steward enjoyed a style of living that was as unpredictable as Lee had expected — a tilted structure, three stories tall, at the edge of town. The man had recently been whitewashing, apparently, but had so done it so haphazardly that the very shrubbery was frosted with it and several of the windows made opaque. (Lee also found paint on several of the cats that passed freely in and out of the home.) It seemed inapposite to Lee that this long-headed man, so stately in dress and gracious in his movements, should now be down on all fours planting seeds in a space not much larger than a newspaper.

"Howdy," Lee said.

"Oh, say! Pefley, is it? And did you bring any little gifts for me perhaps? No?"

Lee blushed. "No funds."

"No, of course not. And yet you seem to be carrying a carton of brand-new cigarettes!"

"I lost that book you loaned me."

"Oh? And which book was that, I wonder?"

Lee now supplied the name of the title and author, mentioning at the same time that it had included a superb woodblock engraving frontispiece picturing a Sixteenth-century ocean scene with a frigate being towed by whales. The man listened patiently, nodding from time to time as Lee described, with growing excitement, certain other elements featured in the engraving.

"Yes? But I wouldn't say you 'lost it' exactly. 'Stolen,' I would have said. Or 'purloined'—probably I would have said that. Purloined by one of the betas and thrown into the lake. And to think that you hiked all this way to tell about it! Would you care for a glass of wine?"

Lee, who had but small experience with wines, acceded to it. He was just now coming to realize that this three-story dwelling and its owner sat athwart one of the most fraught views in the county. Down below, he saw where two rivers threatened to come together but then had failed to do so, forming instead a highly defensible position that obviated any need to repair the broken tower that lay in pieces at the foot of the hill. Shielding his eyes, Lee saw how winter had devastated the plums, blackened the scuppernongs, and scattered large numbers of sweet gum balls all about.

"I have the book, of course."

"Have it!" Lee cheered.

"Why, yes. It had fallen to the bottom of the lake, but then, being the gentlemanly sort of lake that he is, he cast it back up again!" He smiled, making a gracious gesture with a hand that belonged rather to an orchestra conductor than to someone rooting about in the dirt. No doubt he had been a handsome man at one time; unfortunately, when he smiled, it uncovered a set of highly variegated teeth of which some had turned to quartz, and some to other materials.

"What are you planting?"

"Tulips! Yea, and roses, too."

"Won't grow in winter time."

There followed a long and highly awkward silence. Finally, the man began very carefully and slowly extricating the seeds on the tip of his wetted finger and returning them to the envelope. Lee expected now to be led into the house for wine; instead they sat, both of them gazing down into the ravine where a woman in galoshes was hanging clothes out on a line. Lee was disappointed that the man made no protest when one of the little kittens came along and then urinated in installments upon the rather elegant hand with which he supported himself in the painted grass.

"Ah, Lee," he said, "these lovely views. To me it has the ambiance of old Mycenaean Phithia, with Achilles off at war. See that agriculturalist down yonder? He doesn't know what to do—look at him, is he drunk? — what to do with his great lord having been absent for so long."

Not drunk, the agriculturalist was simply having trouble loading his little cart with the neatly-sawed cubes of peat he was heaping upon it. Watching him, and seeing how he had to stop every twenty feet or so and hurry back to retrieve a cube, and seeing further that he had tassels on his cap and was fitted out in a codpiece of some kind…

"Lee! Am I to be held responsible for what happened a thousand years ago on other planets, huh?"

"Naw. Heck, no."

"And Lee! Does it really matter if he should, or should not, arrive home with all his cubes intact? Or that his wife loves him not? Or that it rain one day but not the next? Or the next, Lee, but not today? Hm?"

Lee began to squirm. Suddenly, the inspiration came to him to ask this:

"Say, how come you got fired from so many jobs?"

"So. Talking to Arnsdorf — is *that* how you pass your time? Ah, Lee, I speak the blatant truth when I say that I cannot honestly remember whether it were four jobs and three wives, or four wives and…"

"Three."

"… jobs."

Lee nodded. Down below in the ravine, some three or four children in pantaloons were playing with sticks and hoops, a scene that transfixed the steward and had him close to tears.

"Lee! Ah so, yes. And yet, they too… No, I picked this site on purpose, Lee, just so I could watch what happens in the gulch."

"And how come you quit writing books?"

"Arnsdorf said that? Well, you must appreciate that after a certain time had gone by, and never having actually met anyone I would want for a reader… Excluding you, of course! Ah, Lee. The books, the books did well, but *I* was remaindered." And then in a darker voice: "If you come to me, Lee, it means that you have begun to germinate. That's understandable. And yet the day will come — and you must give me credit for having been the first to find this out — the day when you will never feel alone, save when alone with others. And that will show that you have begun to progress at last. Yes, we've waited a long time for this, Lee, your progression. And you do need to progress, little boy, if you expect to grow hard and cold and learn to deal with publishers."

The house was dim — Lee had forecast that it would be. Barn-like in many ways, he expected to find cats in the kitchen and parrots in the pantry; instead, once his eyes had focused, he discovered the place so crowded with books, with hundreds here and thousands there and dozens more where once there might have been room enough for sitting on the couch, so crowded that Lee began to fear the whole structure might crash down on top of them. That was when the librarian whipped out a flashlight and aimed it into the corner where yet another stack of books reached all the way to the ceiling and participated in holding up the roof. Among it all, Lee saw great volumes and wee ones, but especially a massive tome bound in pigskin that was larger than the man's whole garden and had Yale's insignia on the spine.

"Ah, Lee," he said, "I have tried so hard to bring together here, for you and me, a hoard of books in which it should be possible to verify each single citation in Burton's *Melancholy*. Or fail to verify. Myself, I've found two errors already."

"Two!" Lee smote himself on the forehead. "But have you read *that* one yet?" he asked, pointing toward the giant book.

"Read? Ah, Lee, I've read them all. Or rather, all of them have parts and places that have been read, if not by me, at least by others." Suddenly he hefted up one of the volumes, opened it at hazard and, pointing at the text with his flashlight, began reading aloud in a morose voice from what Lee gathered to be, if not Greek precisely, then one of the other antique languages. Thus passed nine minutes, Lee assimilating none of it.

"Ah, Lee, that was good –to hear again that dear old tongue that no one dares utter anymore. Three books only, that's all I have in Cherokee. Remember, my young friend, that the classification of writers tends to break down between good ones and bad. Now, your bad writers, they…"

Lee nodded sadly.

"… tell about what people do with their hands. Your good writers — and I used to be one — they prefer to delve about in their own single souls. Not afraid to get dirty, those!"

Lee looked at the man's hands, which still had some of the garden on them.

"Ah, Lee, what, really, have we to do, you and me, with what people do to each other?"

Saying nothing, Lee followed him into the next room, where an array of flasks and retorts and a glass-covered set of scales were set out upon a long, narrow table that extended on into the dark. Some of the flasks had corks in them, while from others came an uncanny assortment of odors that percolated throughout the house. Suddenly, Lee jumped back, amazed and horrified to find a dissected cat lying on its back in a bath of formaldehyde. He was happy to move on to the adjoining room, where the man maintained a bindery of some type and where almost at once he spied the drowned book drying over a hotplate with blotters between the pages.

"It's got an engraving in it," Lee said, pointing to the thing.

"Yes! I know."

"A pretty good one, too."

"An excellent one."

They grinned at each other. Never had Lee come up against a person of like temperament. *Now* should be the time for wine, now that they were in agreement about the book.

"Any man who loves books less than human beings... Well! I wouldn't counsel you to have anything to do with a person like that."

"No, sir. Dr. Arnsdorf now, he..."

"Yes, yes, he has books. But stay away from him Lee, that's my final behest."

Lee looked away.

"All right, don't 'stay away from him' exactly—I don't mean it literally. But testy! It's a testy, testy man, Lee, of whom we speak."

"I know."

"'God of Beauty', indeed! I tell you, Leland, if that one had his way, it would mean perpetual war between us here, you and me, and those others down in the village. Wait! Don't misunderstand me, boy; it's not that I'm opposed to war, not if I thought we could win."

"We can't win?"

"Oh, Lee. Oh no, no, no, not ever. No, you must attune yourself to it. Strive to be a zero—I did—and learn to make yourself invisible."

Invisible! Lee, his excitement growing, looked back at the man's chemicals and glassware, and the twenty-gallon flask burbling over a blue-green flame.

"And if wide sleeves be the fashion, then look to your own! Learn to love the theory that is most in vogue at any moment. The economy, Lee—cheer for it. And for the home team. Remember that all men are equal, or that they're not, or that women ought to rule, or ought not — really, does it matter what comes up next? Do all this, Lee, and hew to what the country believes that it believes. Nod more vigorously. Do all this, Leland, and if you be lucky, very, very so, why then…"

Lee waited for it.

"…why then, O Lee, why then you may think your thoughts and read your books and not be made to apologize for it more than once or twice a day!"

Lee clapped his hands.

"And when it comes to choosing a home, select a high place, Lee."

"Like this place?"

"And Lee!"

"Sir?"

"Strive daily to maximize the time that you are not in the presence of others."

Lee, good at taking hints, got up to leave.

"No, no, not *you* Lee; you're welcome here. Small as you are, there's little danger you'll be colliding into my books, knocking them over. Furthermore you seem to navigate very well in all this dim. Better even than Philip, I would say. I do wish you wouldn't smoke, however. Tell me, have you consulted lately with Goldman?"

"A little bit."

"Don't turn your back on that one, Leland; remember that he didn't earn the money himself. No, it came down to him through his fathers." And then in a darker voice: "No one knows how long that money will last, the cost of books being what it is."

"Yes, sir. What will happen when…?"

"What will happen when the sun exhausts its fuel? Bad day, Lee."

But here Lee raised his hand. "Yes, sir. But if the sun…"

"Then there will be no 'day,' properly speaking. Yes, we know you're clever, Lee; you don't have to be proving it all the time. And now I believe I will allow you to depart." (No wine.) "Even friendship is a form of collectivism, after all. And besides, I'm depressed and must lie down."

Lee nodded, backtracking through the darkened room and then wading out through a mélange of cats and kittens. Outside, the sun was blinding to him at first, until he saw that it was simply ordinary weather shifting over into afternoon. And yet it *was* a lovely day.

Eleven

Lee was both humming and talking, both running and stopping every few moments to tie his shoe when, at that moment, the geology professor stepped out in front of him and made it necessary either to run past him or else to stop yet again.

"Lemund?"

Lee looked up at him. The man was dressed in his gemology glasses, which had an eyepiece affixed to the lens. He also carried a geologist's pick, the point bent over from too much use. "Sir?"

"Your shoes — they're no good. And your socks — they're no good, either. And your hair!"

Lee now reached up and touched his hair, a project made more difficult by the extreme size of his head, the unintended result of too much wisdom too abruptly obtained. In fact, he had to stand on tip-toes to find where his head at last came to an end.

"We don't ask," the man went on, "that our boys bathe each single week, no. But in your case..."

"Too cold."

"What?"

"Yeah, and when you walk back, you get your feet all dirty, too."

"Walk back?"

"Yes, sir. From the lake."

"Jove!"

They gathered at the professor's automobile, a black one with a radio in it, and after a long struggle with the ignition, headed out toward the so-called "Chaldean Portal," a massive gate whose inch-thick bars were spaced much too far apart ever to have kept Lee sequestered within the institution's 90 acres. Fifteen times, perhaps more — that's how often he had wriggled through to the outside world each time the village and his enduring need for cigarettes called to him. But never had he traveled as slowly as this, in the company of a man whose notions of time were perhaps too geological for Lee's patience.

"Say, how come you carry all these rocks around with you?" he asked. "And shovels and stuff?"

"And bones? It was good of you, Lee, not to mention those."

He asked no further questions. So many weeks had gone by since he had last traveled an ordinary highway that he found himself striving to learn all he could about each individual car and driver, and indeed, all individuals of any kind. Had clothing styles changed in any significant way during his absence? Turning and shielding his eyes, he studied the woman who was riding stride for stride with them, a middle-aged sort of person who had burst a pimple and had a little tad of toilet paper sticking to her face.

It was a bad day when he had to enter Birmingham with his exaggerated head, his torn trousers, and his shoes in poor condition, very bad. And then to complete the errands that needed to be done and come out again in safety while monitoring the rather naïve man at his side — was he capable of this? Thinking of it, he hurriedly lit a cigarette, but then almost at once snuffed it out again when he saw he already had one between his lips. A bad day and yet, slowly and slowly, the landscape was having its effect. He saw a ruined barn in which a lone mule was holding out in stubbornness against its own impending obsolescence, its Lee-size head framed within a tiny space. The two o'clock sun was three-quarters full and even the missing slice had left a ghost behind. Of crows, Lee saw one only. Stately, wide-awake and proud, the thing stood staring straight ahead while riding on the haunches of a cow. As to the rivers they crossed and the kudzu-strangled pines, Lee was accustomed to that. What shocked and perturbed him, and made him admit that he had been reading too much, was to find amethysts taller than mountains sitting out in the fields, and emeralds, too, that only just now were beginning to melt down beneath December's warmth into those multifarious lakes and ponds that, in times to come, would give delight to those with the eyes to see them.

Those were not emeralds that he saw in Birmingham, but grey buildings full of windows, each window with a face in it, each face putting on an expression of hilarity as Lee came riding in. A long time had gone by since he had last visited this particular city. The geologist said:

"Observe how the little people, being little, how they cluster together for warmth! Thus they build cities. And there, those shacks over yonder, they appear actually to be leaning up against each other!"

It was true. Joined at roof and gable, the buildings formed a consolidated maze that none but those who paid rent could enter. He saw a woman standing in an upstairs window who vanished before Lee could push his cigarette smoke off to one side. A bald-headed man in a bloodstained apron was sweeping in front of his store, while on the corner, two Negroes in loose socks were bending toward the ground, either from stomach cramps or laughing at each other's jokes.

They parked, the professor going to great trouble to position the car in such a way that it pointed straight out of town, in the direction from whence they had come. He said:

"Should we become separated –I don't expect that, but should it happen, why, then run on back here as quick as you can and jump inside. Have the motor running."

"Yes, sir," Lee said, taking care to memorize the location. Without a key, he did not rightly see how he could fire the engine up *or* jump inside. "But what if you don't come back?"

"Lee, Lee. The things that you say!"

It was a weird milieu, here among beggars and drunks and fierce children running up and down. One boy, not much smaller than Lee, was able to throw his top to the pavement and make it spin obediently within an area not much larger than a quarter. Seeing this, the geologist could not but chuckle; Lee watched as he drew out one of his own coins of the same denomination and gave it over to the boy, who saluted and bowed and ended up calling him "squire."

There were so many sights and so much noise that it put a strain on Lee to see and hear it all. He stopped to examine an elderly man dressed in a fez who sat sucking upon a water pipe with a seven-foot-long hose. Coming nearer, Lee looked down into the porcelain bowl that held a full bushel of tobacco mixed with oats. He counted a dozen potters displaying their wares to the northern tourists, dislocated people trying to use their accents in this locality. Behind him, one of the farmers had gotten into a quarrel with a juggler, an emaciated sort of person who had snatched up four of the man's sweet potatoes and was practicing with them. Lee and the professor walked past all this, into a region of coffee merchants offering little piles of brown and black beans arrayed for viewing on brightly-colored quilts that were also for sale. Then came a gawky boy with protruding teeth vending hot mince pies with steam escaping through the fork holes. It aggrieved Lee, to be so devoid of funds.

He refused to look at the girls, especially the black-headed wench in the violet scarf who sat chatting gaily with another girl whom Lee also refused to notice. As for the older women, he looked at them a little bit, concluding that their make-up was perhaps excessive and their voices too sharp. A minute of this and he was ready to revert to the young ones, knowing in his mind that soon they, too, would be excessive in jewelry, voices, and girth. He had not realized the professor was standing just behind him.

"I see what you're doing," the man said.

Lee jumped back. "Sir?"

"Girls. And you seem particularly interested in…this one!" He thought at first that the geologist might actually go and touch her on the nose; instead, he simply adjusted the apparatus affixed to his glasses and inspected the girl at great length with his jeweler's eye. "Oh, yes, I know all about it — girls, youth, all. Come, Lee, we need to talk."

He reluctantly followed to one of the coffee booths that proved to already have a girl in it. The second booth was empty, apart from a lipstick-stained napkin and a cup with tea grounds in it. That was when the proprietor, a hard-looking man with an impairment of some kind, arrived suddenly with two large tumblers of ice water and threw them down in front of Lee and the scientist. Lee now waited for the words — and he knew they were coming — of the person seated across from him.

"Lee?"

"Sir?" He looked up.

"In the matter of girls…"

"Yes, sir."

They drank. The water was better than it appeared and had come to them at minimal cost. Lee now attempted to light a cigarette, but halted suddenly when he perceived yet another girl in the next booth, this one with a diamond anklet that stuck out into view.

"Tell me, Lee, when you're finished."

"Finished?"

"Girl in the next booth."

"I'm finished."

"Good. Now Lee, I…"

"I was only looking!"

"Good! I want you to. The precedent for that is long, Lee, and goes back to the Babylonians."

"Yes, sir." He was being distracted by one of the countrymen, a lantern-jawed personality who had come to town with a brace of geese. But now one goose had slipped its leash and, imagining itself airborne, was running down the aisle with both eyes squeezed tight in a kind of lewd delight.

"Finished with the goose?"

"Yes, sir."

"Good! Now Lee, in the matter of gypsies, you *are* allowed to look."

Lee brightened.

"Girls — remember this, Lee — girls who wear gewgaws about their legs, such girls, Lee, do *not* hate to be looked upon."

Lee nodded. All his life he had suspected something of this kind.

"You see *me* wearing a gewgaw about my…?"

"No, sir," Lee said, checking for it.

"Good! Now Lee, I'd buy that girl for you if I could and take her back to…." He mentioned one of the names of the academy. "But I can't."

"No, sir. Anyway it's the other one, the one over there." He pointed. From this perspective she looked especially good, the sun having cooperated to reveal how glossy her hair was.

"Yes! You wouldn't last ten seconds. But yes, you show good taste, I'll admit that. Strawberries and cherries with ice cream on top — is that how it seems to you at age fourteen?"

"No, sir."

"No?"

"I'm thirteen."

"Ah, Lee. Lee, Lee, Lee. Another two years and you'll be floating in your own semen. What to do?"

"I don't know," he said sincerely.

Together they meditated on it. Of girls, he knew only that some enjoyed being looked upon, a lesson from the geologist's mouth; he had learned it only just a moment ago. And yet except for that, he knew more of philosophy and horses than of girls. That was when his favorite of them, the glossy-headed quantity in the opposite booth, arose and, after adjusting the bright blue ribbon in her own blue-black hair, began to move off (and somewhat arrogantly, too) in the worst of all possible directions, *away* from Lee.

"She's leaving," he reported.

"Indeed?"

"The pretty one."

"Well, that's no good. Here, I'll pay while you go after her. Don't worry, I'll catch up."

Mostly it was the blue ribbon he kept in mind as he trailed after her, visiting the places she visited and modeling his gait upon her own. While it was difficult in the beginning, he quickly acquired the secret of it, namely to lift and bounce and then, at every fifth or sixth step, to turn and throw a smile at whomsoever might be nearest. This one had *not* been reading too much and her face, when he could see it, showed neither thought nor troubles nor any hint of heavy assignments hanging over her head.

He estimated her as being perhaps two years older than himself, old enough to kiss. Not that he durst take hold of her as yet, not while she was tripping along in front of him at a space of about fifteen yards. But where was the scientist, and why had he not come to Lee's assistance?

He chased her, Lee did, around the corner and back again, his two arms growing weary from being held out constantly in the embracing position. Only once did he draw near enough to hear the girl speaking. And if the voice was good, or relatively so, he liked her eyes even better. Two in number, they darted excitedly as she spoke. (Of legs and the rest, he could see almost nothing.) That was when the paleontologist came running up.

"Leland, my boy! Did you…? But where…?"

He pointed to the girl, who dawdled nearby with her comb and compact. Nothing surprised Lee anymore, not even when the man extracted his wallet, drew out his cash and counted it, and then went forward to address the girl. Having spotted the money, the vendors at once began to gather about them, thrusting their various types of merchandise upon the man and boy. The girl herself was gone, or most of her anyway. For he could still now and again catch glimpses of her sky-blue ribbon making briefer and briefer appearances as she entered deeper and deeper into the crowd that opened to receive her.

On many occasions, Lee had heard of the adventures that had befallen his grandfather in this same city in earlier times. That was why he strode forward as hurriedly as he did, ignoring inessential things while keeping a bright eye out for the class of city dwellers who liked to take advantage of people. And that was why he behaved as he did, especially when the seismologist led him off into a clothing store and, after holding up various pairs of trousers and shirts, had him stand in front of a multi-angled mirror that allowed Lee to simultaneously keep watch on all corners of the store at the same time.

He was sent to the dressing room four times, a cell not much larger than a closet, with a great many telephone numbers on the wall. Slowly, reluctantly, Lee tried on all sort of things, until he had at last put together an ensemble that was neither too short nor the other way around. His patience almost at an end, he said nothing when the haberdasher then tried to foist a tie off on him as well, a green one with the picture of a moose on it. He let them do as they must — *his* eye was for the window and the possibility of girls passing by.

The geologist paid out of a purse that also held a few snail-like fossils smaller than dice. Lee strode vigorously about the shop, striving in vain to accustom himself to the barking of his new shoes and his own extra half-inch in height. Soon enough, the shoes were traveling "of themselves," and promptly carried him outside.

They wandered far, the topographer and Lee, penetrating even into the massive pediment of the monstrous *Hephaestus*, a mile-high statue made of chromium and bismuth and said to have been a gift from one of the South American tyrants who had once passed a summer in this town in his youth. Here among the restaurants and the shops, among tourists and guards, they came upon a tiny bookstore so full that the three of them, Lee, a woman, and the geologist, had scarcely room enough to open the books and try them out without at the same time clashing elbows with each other. All this faded into unimportance, however, when Lee laid eyes for the first time upon a brilliant book jacket of many colors that showed a man holding two enormous crocodiles at bay with an ordinary pocket knife. He pounced upon it at once and began splashing through the pages in search of those other illustrations he felt sure the book contained. Already he had singled out a paper-bound copy of one of Schopenhauer's lesser works, simply trusting to it that the professor was as able to pay for these as for the clothes that Lee had not really wanted in the first place.

Each man chose two books. Keeping an eye out for girls, Lee followed from the shop and then began to ascend a spiral staircase into the upraised arm of the monument, a tube-like passage congested not with bones and veins, but cables rather, and clusters of electrical wiring that Lee was careful not to touch. Mounting past a narrow window, he caught sight of the deity's face, a half-acre of pure hauteur, and of his enormous hammer visible between the clouds. To this dangerous perch he, Leland Pefley, was steadily climbing while knowing full well the consequences to him and to others should that brawny man at last bring down his dread mallet onto the "anvil" that was Birmingham itself. It didn't bear thinking about. Thinking about it, Lee left off reading. No girls — none would come *this* high.

They arrived at a restaurant in the open sky. Amazed, charmed, excited, Lee counted six tables squeezed into a small area, each table covered with a cloth that bore the name in golden thread of the "Vulcan," as the Birminghamians had named him.

"Shall we dine?"

Lee, putting on a bored expression, was not averse to it. The place had no girls in it, nor any others except for an elderly couple who gazed upon them with disapproval. Lee stood and bowed sweepingly to them. His shoes were new, his tie as well, and he saw no reason why people should be displeased with them, which is to say unless it was because the geographer was muttering too loudly as he reviewed the menu through his jeweler's scope.

"Leland?"

"Sir?"

"Why are we here?"

Lee thought about it.

"We are here, Leland, in this *expensive* place" — he mentioned these last words very loudly while at the same time casting a hard glance at the waiter, a lordly man in a scarlet jacket who did, in truth, somewhat resemble the deity he was serving — "this *most expensive* of all places…"

Lee waited for it.

"… in order to celebrate the birth last week of a truly great geologist."

"Yes, sir. Who is it?"

"Well! We don't yet know, do we? But when you are fifty, or sixty mayhap, *then* you'll know who it was."

"Yes, sir, I reckon." He added: "But you won't."

"Leland! Was that kind? The truth is, I expect to endure until I'm ninety."

Lee nodded dubiously and looked off into the sky that surrounded them on three sides.

"And how do I know that? Is that your question?"

"Yes, sir."

"Why, because I used to be a progressive, Leland, and passionate about it, too. But then I came to age forty-five—and I remember the very hour—and found that I had been transformed into a reactionary! How do you explain that?"

"Well, I guess..."

"Because, Leland, because at age forty-five, I realized all of a sudden that I had a shrinking future and... Yes?"

"You had a..."

"Yes?"

"... your future..."

"Don't stop now!"

"Your past was getting bigger but...."

"Excellent! Just excellent! And someday you'll have a larger past than future, too."

Lee blushed modestly. The waiter had arrived, bringing a tray with two goblets on it. Lee reached for the one with the pale green contents, but after receiving a slap on the wrist, ended up with the juice instead.

"Leland?"

"Sir?"

"You want the *true* truth?"

"I guess."

"We're actually here to celebrate what you have achieved in Greek. Why, you're almost as good at that stuff as... What's his name?"

"Philip," Lee said.

They had a superior meal even if, to Lee's thinking, the quality of it had militated against the quantity, leaving him with a fork in one hand and his eye upon the kitchen. Since there were no girls, he glanced instead at a fat man in an undershirt, washing dishes in a tub of suds. Finally, admitting to himself that the meal was finished, he pushed back and ignited a cigarette. Across from him, the white-haired man sat staring back through the apparatus attached to his double-glazed lenses held in a mahogany frame. He had taken one of his just-purchased books and had opened it to a colored photograph of a surgical procedure, a ghastly picture showing the person's innards.

"Now Lee, next time you find yourself thinking about things, just open to this page"—he handed the book over to him—"and see for yourself what girls are actually made of. That ought to calm you down for a while."

Lee took it, but trained his eyes on the margins of the page.

"Thanks a lot," he said.

The afternoon drew on, but neither of them was ready to abandon the place. Lee could see all the way to Tennessee, a gracious land, he believed, where people were waltzing their lives away.

"Did you know, Lee," the man asked, "that at one time, a man could get a living by herding sheep, or piloting ships?"

"Or," Lee said, "fishing for fish."

"Applying gold dust to the fore-edges of books? Coordinating the activities of bees? Tin smithing?"

"Yes, sir." He was sitting on the book, hoping never to see it again.

"But now we're far beyond all that, Lee. Nowadays a man can grow up to be an analyst or broker, or serve as a consultant to a public relations firm. See how far we've come?"

Lee marveled.

"But do you know, Leland, what it means to live in an *authentic* democracy?"

Lee raised his hand to answer, but then slowly drew it down again.

"Where we'd all be skinned and boiled, folks like you and me, if the people thought it might increase the economy by half a pence, or improve the batting average of the home team. And you, Lee, do you really want to give your life to what the democracy believes to be a waste of time? Go home, boy, go now, 'afore it's too late!"

"Can't."

"Can't?"

"No, sir."

"Oh, dear."

They both smoked at length, each thinking his own thoughts until, at a little past four in the afternoon, the waiter came out with a dish of cherries and strawberries covered in several kinds of ice cream. So this was Lee's reward for having a head for details (and Greek was full of these), and for his ability to stay up late at night. Lee jumped into the stuff at once, but then decided to prolong the pleasure for as long as possible. It gave the geologist all the time he needed to browse through Lee's crocodile book.

"Pefley," he said, "you've got ten seconds. And then I'm going to throw that slop over the side."

Ten seconds were enough. In his haste he had dropped his Schopenhauer book on the floor, a fate that would not have surprised its author. Lee salvaged it and then, taking a cigarette, stood and sauntered out onto the balcony from whence a dozen counties could be seen spread out below them, their outlandish names (derived mostly from Choctaw and Chickasaw) drawn in mile-high captions that ran up and down the rather complicated terrain. The Alabamas he beheld in their entirety, the South made whole and, just beneath them, 10,000 admiring girls — he wanted to fertilize every one of them — in the form of pedestrians hurrying back and forth.

"Arrogance, Lee, it sticks out all over you. Tsk, tsk, tsk. I see enemies in your future, Lee, many."

But Lee, who really preferred to be alone when these moments came over him, didn't speak. Of those faraway volcanoes said to be "extinct," he could see that at least one of them had begun smoldering again. Looking next toward Europe, he identified where, on the eastern horizon, there still subsisted the once-famous islands of Brittany and France. He saw more, including a spate of tiny dots representing the triple-masted ships that someday would carry him there. Suddenly, the sun blinked off and the world turned dark for a moment — was he the only one to have noticed?

"Lee!"

So they dawdled there. The waiter himself had long ago given up on them and gone away. Once, but once only, the giant bronze statue made a creaking noise that Lee ascribed to the normal contractions of metal when winter is coming in. (Of the god's face, he had to lean out perilously over the railing to get even the merest look at it. Years later, he was still to remember it, a countenance that might almost have been noble or even divine, before that effect had been vitiated by high-powered rifles and lightning strikes. Just then, Lee realized that the professor had been speaking to him for the past minute.)

"Lee? Do you see this paper napkin that I hold here in front of your eyes? Let it represent the work of the mind and soul within the context of democracy. Good! And here, this tiny little chit that I've just now torn from the corner — let this represent the regard that people in the outside world are inclined to give to such efforts. Are you the man to endure a disparity like that?"

Lee took the chit over into his own hands, turning it over twice and marveling at it and then, when the man was no longer watching, putting it away in his vest.

From there, they walked hurriedly across town, probing into various shops for the oil, salt, kerosene and ammunition needed by the institution. They bought thirty batteries, six of them strong. They shopped for antifreeze, toothpaste, certain basic medicines and six quarts of ink.

Thirty batteries they bought, but no girls, six of them strong.

Twelve

Having passed the next several days in silence, Tuesday came up all too suddenly, a dark, leering, and dangerous time so gloomy that Lee had trouble finding his way. Once before, he had seen clouds of this type, disembodied brains thinking philosophic thoughts. So had it been on the day that Ctesiphon fell, with nothing to look forward to except hundreds of years of darkness at night and dimness by day — such was Lee's historical knowledge.

To start, he went straight to the man's private office, an L-shaped demesne cluttered with fishing tackle, empty bottles, and stand-up portraits of the little brown-headed woman who had served as his wife. Here, Lee sat and waited while playing with his cigarettes and humming, in a barely audible voice, the song called "Long Ago and Far Away." Nothing surprised him anymore, and if he must be expelled from the academy, or sent to join the gammas, as the less worthy students were called, he was prepared for that as well. That was when the stenographer peeped in.

"Leland? Oh, no, Mr. Goldman wants you to come to the lake. Weren't you told?"

Lee ran. He had not been told about the lake, and if he was to be chided, let it be on account of something of importance and not mere tardiness. Arriving from the east, Lee soon found the man, covered in gloom, gazing out over the water with a toy telescope that was slenderer than all but one of his fingers. The boy approached in silence, eyes cast down in modesty.

"You!"

"I came."

"Late, you're late. Quite late."

"Yeah, but…!"

"No! No excuses, please. I'm just simply not in the mood for them." (Lee made no remark about the dozen or so letters in his lap, old ones, to judge by the postage and deteriorating ink.) "Tell me, are you getting enough to eat these days?"

"No, sir."

"Because we've decided to let you stay."

"Sir?"

"No, no, you don't have to thank me. We aren't doing it for you, after all, but rather for…" His voice ground to a halt when he spotted three swans encroaching slyly to shore. He tried to bring them nearer with coos and endearments, but then suddenly took something from his briefcase and hurled it at them.

"Well?"

"Sir?"

"Is there nothing you wish to say?"

"Yes, sir! Thanks."

"It doesn't come free, you understand."

Lee agreed.

"Well?"

"Sir?"

"Well, my God, aren't you even going to ask why?"

"Yes, sir!"

"It was my decision."

"Oh," said Lee.

"They're *all* my decisions, as far as the eye can see. All seven hundred acres. You see that tower up yonder? The ruint one on Mahler's Hill?"

"Yes, sir."

"That's *not* my decision. No, that's state property."

"I know."

"And yet you've been up there, haven't you? Forcing my poor horsie up those awful slopes."

Lee looked down. "Once."

"No, several times. And how often, Leland, have you forced the miserable thing to go swimming with you"—he touched it with his pole—"in this very lake? Why, I've seen it with my own eyes!"

Lee continued to look down.

"Anyway, we've decided to let you stay, Arnsdorf and me. And that other fellow—what's his name? That book person. Watch it!"

Again he hurled, this time catching the most presumptuous of the swans with a glancing blow. Only now was Lee able to see what he was using for ammunition, pricey stuff, one would have thought, to be using as missiles.

"We didn't bring you here, Lee, so you could make a name for yourself and prance about in view of the people, no, nor so you could become a Senator or millionaire."

"No, sir."

"You've noticed how those barracks of yours keep on losing tenants? *They* wanted to be Senators and millionaires. Or rather, their parents would have wanted it, had we given them a vote in the matter. I tell you, Lee, you hear of any of *my* boys doing well in this society and you'll know that I have failed."

Lee nodded and drew out the little notebook that he carried at all times. His pencil was blunt enough, certainly, and yet he was still able to transcribe the man's words, or most of them at any rate.

It's equality we seek here, Lee. Equality, equality, equality, always in equal degree. Oh! But did I tell you that we prefer it without the 'e'?"

Lee went back and erased that particular letter.

"My daddy! He'd be pissing all over hisself, if he could see me spending his beloved money on Edmund and you and... What's his name?"

"Philip," said Lee.

An hour and twenty minutes went past, Lee taking his turn at the fishing rod while the Director napped. Just fourteen weeks ago, Lee had been adept at this, but now his skill had apparently abandoned him. He even tried to exert his Will upon the fish, a wasted effort that brought only seaweed to the surface. Thus far that Will of his had only proved effective *vis-à-vis* the sun.

"You'll be eating a lot better now," the man said, once he had recovered from his snooze. "Now that we're rid of all those gammas and so on."

"Yes, sir; I'd like to get rid of a lot more of 'em, too, if I had my way."

"I know you would. And I expect you'd purge us all the way down to just one little student if you could. Am I right about that, Lee? One?"

"Philip now, he..."

"No, no, and again no! Why, I'm more likely to purge you than him! So just hush about it."

"Yeah, but...."

"No! I want me all the Philips I can get. Thousands, if I knew where to find 'em — cold boys full of brains. He doesn't seem to have a single friend anywhere, so far as I can tell. You, on the other hand, have been seen talking to Young Mecham."

Lee again looked down.

"Yes, he'll go far, that one. And did you know the little son-of-a-bitch has taken up Chinese? It's true, of course, that he's hopeless when it comes to carpentry or welding or"—he glanced at Lee—"horsemanship."

"Yeah, and I'm lots better than he is in abstract concepts, too. Dr. Spivey said so."

"Oh? Well, I think *you're* an abstract concept Lee. Why, I doubt if anyone like you has ever actually existed! Except on paper, of course. What, you want me to put that boy up against the wall and shoot him? That what you want?"

Lee, hopeful at first, saw that the man was not really serious. For one, fleeting moment, he was tempted to tell about it—how on a certain afternoon he had remained beneath water while Philip had progressively weakened and, finally, come up for air.

"If you just knew..."

"And then I'd shoot him? I doubt it."

Always ready to die, it still seemed to Lee that his own methods were nobler than Philip's slightly higher marks in science, math, French, and several other disciplines. Sulking about it, he drew out a torn cigarette and set it on fire. It was true about Philip's chemistry scores—that they were "out of this world," and because nothing was ever better than perfection, nothing was better ever than Philip's scores. But would he have died for them?

"Yeah, but would he of died for 'em?"

"Drop it, Lee. Remember you still have... Why, you little son-of-a-bitch! You dare to smoke in my presence? Moses! First you purge me of my best student and then you light up a goddamn cigarette! Curse you, boy."

In the afternoon, three crows flew over. Lee watched as, casting lustful glances down upon the swans, they turned and came back again. The day was dark, darker than before, and with numerous thick clouds lying atop each other like sediment in the sky. Goldman stirred and snorted, began scratching his testicles and grabbing for his fishing pole.

"You will have noticed, Lee," he said, "how the ordinary man, being ordinary, how he seeks for something grand to cling to—have you noticed that?"

"Yes, sir; I notice it all the time."

"We are surrounded by patriots, my boy." He motioned around at the hills. "A small people getting continually smaller, sports fans and voters and the like. Imagine when they find at last that they've only been clinging to so many other small ones just like themselves!" And then more darkly: "Stay away from power, Lee. Remember, there's no glory to be had in lording it over betas and gammas and the like."

Lee wrote it down.

"Power, Lee, power, fame and influence — it all lies within the gift of the people, and therefore has no value."

"Nothing surprises me anymore."

"Here, Lee, we sing the aristocracy that is hard, so very hard to enter."

"Boy howdy it is!"

"And so easy to be expunged. Three hundred years of history, Leland, and not one single man of genius. In the European sense, I mean."

Lee looked at him severely for the space of a few seconds, until at last the man relented:

"Oh, all right, I *will* exempt Poe. But no one else!"

"It begins with compassion," the man said later, after the second of his naps, "and ends in goo. And then, next thing, they'll be collectivizing not just possessions, Lee, but souls. Oh Lee, Lee, Lee, we're surrounded by progressives here, and similar types." (He indicated the same hills that only a moment ago had been full of patriots and small people.)

"Surrounded, yes, sir."

"Because your progressive, Lee, only loves those who stand below him in the scale of things. Remember! Nothing so infuriates a progressive as the sight of someone who doesn't need help. *His* help."

"I'll remember."

"Never, never, never allow yourself to stand in need of help."

"But what if…?"

"Then die!" He stood and hurled, aiming at nothing. Lee saw how the object went sailing for an extraordinary length before it finally slackened and began to sink. And even then it continued to go on for a distance. "And Lee?"

"Sir?" The object had not yet reached the ground.

"I recommend that you permit each ethnic group to form, independently, an experiment of its own. Or Philip, in case the job falls to him — tell him to let each nation work out its own trajectory, each one becoming more isolated, unique and strange. I sing a world of 10,000 states, each weirder than the next. But why did you not bring a better pencil, Lee, to write this down?"

It was near to three in the afternoon before Lee at last cajoled one of the trout into taking the hook. With great pride, he reeled the creature in and held it up in front of the man who sat regarding it sorrowfully.

"To deal with people as if they were equal — could anything be more unjust? Yes, yes, I see it; throw it back. And you needn't put on a face like that — we didn't fetch you here to pester the trout."

At this, Lee jumped up, shouting, "You did! You did so! That man who fetched me here, he said..."

They were distracted by the view of gammas, some six or eight head of them (one head bullet-shaped) shambling down the opposite coast with spades and frows. These days it required two men, one of them armed with a shotgun, to herd them to the fields in the morning and bring them back at a quarter past five. Of this crowd, two were pushing barrows that were loaded, indeed spilling over with potatoes newly excavated out of the wonderful soil that washed down from Mahler's Brow. Lee saw clearly that two of the potatoes had bounced out of the leading barrow, and yet no one had bothered to gather them up. It made his gorge rise.

"Lee?"

"Sir?"

"I don't want you shoveling manure any longer, you hear? We have" — he nodded toward the thralls — "others for that. And besides, the horsie is now yours."

Lee, astounded, stared at him with bulging eyes and then spun about, applauding the man's decision. All anger, all regrets, all speculation that he might really prefer to be somewhere else, all that now fled away.

"What will you name him?"

Lee supplied the appellation, a resplendent one from Hindu literature. The animal was already accustomed to it and to no other.

"Your eighty pounds, he'll like that so much better than my twenty-three and some odd stone. But tell me, Lee, is it true what they say about you? That you go riding every day upon the weald singing 'Long Ago and Far Away'?"

"No, sir!"

"Truly?"

"No, sir! We always stay upon the wold."

Night came. Lee, his possessions augmented by a horse, very much needed to piss, a project that he, unlike the Director, was not willing to perform in open view. For some time, the larger man had been struggling to speak, emitting a popping noise that Lee had pretty much given up trying to interpret. He thought he heard this:

"Canst thrive, Lee, on self alone and be the hero of your own existence? Ecstasize on art? Stand apart as fashions rise and fall? Stay away from universities?"

"I might."

"Well, then!" He rubbed his hands together gleefully. "And so our interview comes to an end. You to go to your place, and I to mine." He pointed toward his place. "However, you may depend upon it that we shall meet at least one more time. Go now!" He sneezed and then added, "But be careful in all this dark."

Alone in his rooms, Lee spent almost half an hour arranging and rearranging the books in his floor-to-ceiling bookcase. Meanwhile, he was listening with attention to the music of the Light Crust Flour Doughboys, despite Arnsdorf's opinion of them. That he now had "rooms," and not just one room only, was owing to the boy who until recently had been his nearest neighbor. Lee had welcomed his expulsion, seizing upon the chance to set up a three-room complex out of the space made available as a result.

Three rooms were better than two. They let him expand his books and collections into more plenteous spaces. Better yet, the expelled boy had enjoyed the use of a carpet so deep and dense that Lee had immediately discovered two pennies in it, cold ones that he had blundered upon with his toes.

He also had a radio, a disembodied sort of thing given to him by the geologist that had lost its housing many years ago. Surrounded by mountains, Lee had found it difficult to tune in to the signals that he assumed crisscrossed overhead and entice them into the box. Fortunately, he had an alternate machine in the corner of his middle room, a gift from Arnsdorf after a particularly heavy meal. Not that Lee could be so easily deceived into listening to the sort of music that man was constantly urging—far from it! No, it was mostly for Philip's ear that he played the stuff night and day. Lee himself was able to ignore it.

Going to his second-best desk, he seated himself and put on a serious expression. But hardly had he read a full page before he had to rise and attend to that third machine of his, a coal-burning stove whose shape and choleric spirit so closely duplicated the music professor's. Now an expert in the use of tongs, he quickly threw in some half-dozen nuggets of fuel and then stood back, hypnotized as the coal began to shift and groan and, finally, suppurate into bright green fire. Frigid night it was; already it had cleared the field of cattle, driven the community's lone hound indoors, and dismissed a very great many erstwhile stars, leaving naught but acres of emptiness in the gingham sky. One such star, it is true, *had* survived, a pitiable thing striving to keep from sputtering out in the breeze. He cheered for it, until he saw that the moon was in an even worse condition, whole provinces having fallen into ruin.

Lee now returned to the center of the room from where he could spy in upon Young Edmund Burchem, bent happily over his desk two doors down. They never spoke anymore, not since the churl had fallen into a mathematics-centered curriculum (designed just for him) and had become hopelessly bogged down in the stuff, becoming more and more cheerful by the month. He whom Lee had formerly patronized was now allowed the foremost place in topology class.

All this faded off into inconsequentiality, however, when compared to Philip's itinerary. Where, really, had this boy come from? From Tennessee, it was said, an oblong state squeezed alphabetically between Texas and some other place that Lee could not immediately name. And the glasses that he wore — whence came *they*? Abandoning the center of his room, Lee inched forward to gain a better view of this person. Flaxen-headed, of ordinary construction both above the neck and below it, the boy had learned to sit with more patience than if he were one of his own sparse pieces of furniture. What, really, were his intentions, sitting like that? And yet the boy's rooms, all five of them, were not, and had never been especially neat and tidy. "*My* rooms," said Lee, speaking to himself, "are incomparably more tidy than his. And I can hold my breath longer, too."

He smoked two cigarettes and read fourteen pages concurrently. His record had finished and, in the silence that followed, he believed it was Philip's pen that he could hear, a small noise that came from just beyond the partition. Most of the other students had gathered in the Great Room, where one of them was reciting one of his own compositions before the fire. Yes, it *was* Philip's pen that Lee had heard—he could recognize the unhurried certainty in the way he pushed the instrument across a sheet a paper, pausing only occasionally to sketch in the most amazing little drawings of a bisected seed, or a word of Greek, or a sidereal view of whichever master might be lecturing at the time. Lee's own drawings were quite worthless, an embarrassment indeed, for which reason he no longer produced any. In any case, he much preferred concepts, and the more abstract they were, the more they called to him and spoke. Philip, on the other hand, was mere trash in the matter of concepts, quite hopeless really, and deserved only to be laughed at. And Lee did laugh, producing a sound of high merriment combined with the most extreme dislike. In the meantime, Young Edmund's room had fallen dark, the door was closed, and the boy inside no doubt asleep by now.

Lee labored on until past midnight, wasting the greater part of his time on two Greek verbs of hideous complexity; not once could he set down the entire conjugation without making at least one error, even were it nothing more than a half-millimeter-long dash or a half-moon sign that sat upon the head of certain letters for purposes still unclear to Lee. It was from having to cope with such a language that the original Greeks had become what they were; as for Lee, he wanted to scream. But just let morning come and Philip will have stored away in the warehouse that was his mind every jot and twiddle of it, even down to the pestilential little "iota subscript" that, provided Lee could have his way, would have been marched into a jar, the jar sealed, and the whole of it drowned in the sea! Instead, he rose and smoked, and then stepped outside for a brief period to sample the texture of the night.

The time having arrived at last, Lee hastened into his pajamas and, taking the candle with him, crawled beneath the bed to verify that the slats were still numerous enough and properly spaced. But even now he could still hear the noise that came from Philip's pen, a stealthy sound that Lee's expert ear, and his only, could distinguish from the noise of rooks whispering in the attic. The slats were good, the rug was deep and the candle was contributing to the warmth. Pleased by it, he decided to remain where he was. And then, in case the gammas snapped their chains… They would just have to go away disappointed, having never thought to look beneath the bed.

Thirteen

He developed, therefore he suffered; these days when he encountered Edmund, it was the smaller boy who was cheerful and Lee who was close to tears.

"You're deteriorating."

"Naw," Lee would say. "I'm just developing a little too fast."

"Careful! Arnsdorf's watching."

They scattered. Over the hill and down by the lake, the remaining boys could be seen coming from different directions, their eyes upon the seven colored pennants furling gaily from the turrets of Flinder Hall. Those streamers represented seven who would be allowed to stay.

Lee preferred to sit in the foremost row, where he could use his Will upon the lecturer while at the same time allowing it to be seen in his face just how well-intentioned he was. Accordingly, he now set about organizing his papers, his ruler, his tobacco and matches and numerous sharp pencils. Suddenly, he jumped back and groaned out loud, recognizing too late that he had placed himself just next to Philip.

The boy was cold and had no nervous habits. His glasses, meanwhile, continued to have that quality about them, as if they had rested overnight in naphtha and then been polished with great patience over a long period of time. It allowed Lee, indeed allowed everyone, to see just how blue, calm, and chilly were that person's actual eyes. As for nervous habits, Lee would have been glad if he himself had fewer than he did. He suddenly reached for a cigarette, knocking over his ink. That was when Arnsdorf came in.

These sessions might go on for three hours or more, the man sometimes speaking, sometimes playing music, and then sometimes inviting his wife to join them, whose voice was superior to his own. And sometimes he trespassed into philosophy, citing it as a sub-division of music itself. Or, he might simply turn up the volume and sit there, head in hands, suffering from Beauty and the migraines the boys inspired in him.

"It galls me," he said, "looking at you and knowing what you are — the loathsome tediousness of youth. Twenty years I foresee, years of getting a living, of house-hunting and house-having, of canoodling with girls. Makes me want to...!"

Lee thought for a moment he might actually vomit; instead, as that moment, his wife came in shyly and then went and stood in the corner. She was a heavy woman, too much so really, but her dress was green and glamorous and made, it seemed, of satin.

"Man," said Arnsdorf, continuing with his talk, "is shit. And whosoever puts shit at the center of things, he builds a system that rests on shit."

Edmund raised his hand.

"Wrong!" said Arnsdorf, preventing the boy from speaking. "Wrong, wrong, wrong! I'm surprised at you, Burchem, a classic error. No mere 'man' wrote these measures. Oh, yes, it is true to be sure that this or that 'man' might now and again serve as the conduit through which Beauty might, for a moment, elect to flow. No? But whether it's this man or that, they all of them deserve our pity."

"Pity!"

"Why, yes, I have said so. And how would *you* like it — to serve out your whole life as Something Else's herald? Or allow Beauty to pierce you in places never meant even to be touched? "

"I would." It was a small voice that came from the back of the room. Outside it had begun to rain, veiling the mountains. Listening to the music and the man and with his attention focused upon the fog-bound mountains, Lee could see that his resistance was breaking down. Whether it was something in Wagner (the "best five hours in human history," as Arnsdorf called it), or whether it was not, this much Lee did understand: that the woman was not going to be allowed to sing after all. He watched sympathetically as, blushing and smiling, she at last withdrew and then set off running through the rain. Never was Lee to forget it — the gown trailing after her, her husband shouting amid the noise, and Lee's resistance crumbling as the music arrived at some of history's best moments.

Fourteen

It was a three-mile jaunt through forest and bramble to a low-lying area where he had to ford the creek; these days he never went out without a book or two, well-jacketed volumes that he could whip out at tremendous speed. His clothes had large pockets in them.

Down along the railroad tracks! Here among the weeds he was able to gather nectar jars with adorable little "corks" in them. Those pods held an uncanny liqueur to which Lee and the hobos were addicted. But mostly he marveled at how such rare and precious things had sprung up *here*, where each passing train represented danger on a regular schedule. Lee, too, he was in danger at all times from the sons of the local peasantry—"clowns," as he had begun calling them—who loved to loiter here while pre-empting the best of the nectar.

The town itself was bleak, nor would Alabama have wanted it any other way. He entered slowly, hat pulled low as he moved as noiselessly as he could past the four dry men sitting shoulder-to-shoulder beneath the awning of the dry goods store. They, as least, suspected nothing of the texts in his pocket, the pods in his vest, or the transformations that had lately taken place in his mental conceptions. Five paces further, he encountered a woman of some thirty or forty years—he knew the type—or possibly of fifty who looked back over her shoulder at him with motherly concern. He bowed, sweepingly. He knew that she would certainly have fled away in horror, stopping her ears, if only she could have seen the tenth part of what was going on inside his head. And yet his face remained quite cheerful!

He limped past the barber's, where there were some half-dozen sullen and self-despising old men encouraging each other with jokes and nods as they listened to imbecility on the radio. No one offered him any trouble, not until he stepped over a slumbering hound who lifted up his head and stared searchingly—these things were smart—into Lee's averted gaze.

He knocked several times, entered, and then went down into the sub-basement and looked about in it for a considerable time before coming back up again and finding the bookman sleeping on a pallet where, until recently, the bathtub had been situated. Lee was loathe to rouse a man who, like himself, slept poorly of nights. Coming nearer, he inspected the man's complexion, a curdled tableau with enlarged pores encapsulating a person who might almost have been handsome at one time. His teeth, poorly moored, had fallen into desuetude and transmogrified into a quartz-like material that sparkled as he snored. Lee bent still nearer, meaning to get a better picture of those "teeth" when, at that moment, the man suddenly sat upright, yelling, "Mother!"

Lee was embarrassed. He tried to cover for it by pulling out one of his books and reading in it.

"Ah! Lee, is it?"

"Yes, sir."

"Very good. Presumably I was sleeping just now and..."

"Yes, sir. I didn't bring any little gifts or presents this time because..."

"Because you have no funds — is that what you mean to say?"

"Yes, sir."

"And yet you manage to keep yourself in cigarettes. How can that be?"

"I don't know."

"Ah, Lee. You passed any number of little stores and shops on your long stroll, delicatessens and so forth. Handicraft outlets. And did you think to ask for credit in just one of those? No."

Lee looked down. "Been doing lots of reading," he said finally, still looking down.

"Oh?"

"Yes, sir. Books."

"Alright, I'll accept that. And what's that I see peeking out of your pocket there? No, no, not that one. That can't be *gold dust* I see! On the fore-edge?"

Lee plucked it out and handed it over. It was not especially remarkable, not as literature; it was, however, one of the handsomest volumes that either man had ever seen. Together they gloated over it, both fighting for the first privilege to crack it open.

"Oh, Lee. Oh, oh, oh. Oh, you'll go far. Just look at that rascal!"

"Can I have it back now?"

"Back?"

"It belongs to Mr. Arnsdorf."

The man growled. Lee did not know whether he had a greater desire to seize the book and be off with it, or whether to continue gazing in fascination at the man's "teeth."

"Ah, Lee. But why oh why do they waste such workmanship upon a… Novel, is it? And by a woman?"

Lee admitted it. Nor had he provided the full truth about the book, which in fact belonged to Arnsdorf's wife.

"Novel, yes, sir. I'll just put it away here in my pocket, OK? So's I can give it back to…"

"Arnsdorf's woman, yes. Coffee, Lee? Or wine?"

"Wine." He waited as the man arose painfully, got into his slippers, and then blundered into the adjoining room where he poured himself—and himself only—a steeping glass of amber-colored wine in which a great many little pieces of cork could be seen rotating wildly.

"Ah, Lee, that was good," he said, blotting his lips with the tail of the curtain. "And now shall we look into my Reformation collection? I have so many fine things. And Lee! Although you may think you know about black ink, I still say you know nothing at all until you have sampled the true German black inks of circa 1525."

Lee followed down into the two-level basement hewn out of red clay and filled with shelving and cabinets of every kind, all of them loaded with provender for that "new world library" being assembled at Goldman's behest. And everywhere that Lee looked, on each box and every shelf, he found the insignia of a certain famous university on everything.

"Lee?"

"Sir?"

"I can't find the Reformation. But say, you like the French Revolution, don't you?"

"I used to. When I was a kid." (In truth, he had been eagerly anticipating the great German black inks of circa 1525.)

"Mayan codices? Oh, these are good, *very* good. Shall I bring them out into the yard? The sun, you understand."

They went up. The man, who was strong, bore the crate with surpassing ease upon his shoulder. It was when they had ascended to the next level that Lee saw, arrayed on the shelves, some hundred or more enormous volumes bound all in membrane and each of them bearing Yale's extraordinary and very gorgeous armorial embossment.

They went out into the light and strode to the bare place where, until recently, the cats had been wont to do their breeding. Lee knew this valley very well by now, knew the barns, the cows, and the colored cottages where dwelled the peasants responsible for this most painterly of scenes. Today each cottage produced a string of smoke lifting whimsically from each teetering chimney.

"Ah, Lee. I've had some of my most original thoughts while gazing down upon these people." He probed into the crate, coming out with the first of the codices and holding it in the light. From his position Lee could see but a single pictogram — that of a boa being consumed by a crocodile. It was, he knew, an important emblem, destined from long ago to become the trademark of a certain well-known brand of grits.

"Ah, Lee, such deities as ruled in those days! See there? Why, that one looks like Goldman! And there! See? They're actually cutting out the poor man's heart! No, no, it's too late, Lee, altogether too late. For even if perfect justice were to prevail hereafter, it's still too late, I say, to abrogate all the horribleness that has taken place in Mexico."

"Nothing surprises me, not anymore."

"Lee! We are surrounded by horribleness!" He pointed toward the village, the cows, and finally to the small brown cat peeping around the corner. "But don't listen to what *I* say. After all, someday you'll be as over-refined as I am, if not more so."

Lee forced himself to pay no notice to the rash of cork crumbs adhering to the man's stubble and lips. Instead he looked to the valley, where two peasant boys were running and calling and chasing hens, just as he himself might be doing, had things been different.

"Ah, Lee, I grow old. And someday, when things are different, you'll grow older, too. But don't speak to me of wives, Lee, though I know you're curious. If they had their way, those wives of mine, they would have sold all my books at auction in a single lot. Yes, and run off with the money, too. No, no, they'll never find me here, not in this... What? Alabama is it?"

"Yes, sir."

"Ah!'

They read until noon, each on his own side of the garden. Glancing up from time to time, Lee sometimes saw the man smiling, while at other times he seemed close to tears. Finally, coming to a halting place (and Lucretius was full of these), Lee called over to him:

"But what about the future?"

"Future? I'm sixty last month. No future. And someday, Lee, you'll have no future, too."

"Yeah, but…"

"Oh, I don't say you won't have your meed of wives and houses, of books clamoring to be writ, and so on, and so on. But remember this — that you'll fall in love for the first time just one time only."

"One!"

"Or none."

Lee reflected on it. "But what kinds of things did you used to do, before you fell in love one time only?"

"Ah, Lee."

He woke at a little past two to find three farm boys in the valley riding on a cow. It was a blustery day, turning chill.

"Ah, Lee. Lee, I've had three good minutes in my life, three in half a century. That's not many!"

"Yes, sir. I can barely hear you, way over here."

"My first good minute? It was a chill day, turning blustery."

"Like this day?"

"Hm? Oh, no, the times that *I* remember happened all long before the health of the West had passed away. And you must realize that, in those days, no one was younger than I. And now, Lee, I must ask you to summon up this picture — the Young Spivey. Playing hard, playing all day, young Spivey in the sun, playing with stick and ball. You know the syndrome."

"Yes, sir."

"Yes, I believe you do! But what it all comes down to is this: that I lay that night beneath a tin roof in endless-seeming rain."

Lee waited for him to go on; instead, the man blushed deeply and began picking at the grass.

"Yes, that's the whole of it. But did I mention about the rain? And the sheets, Lee, the sheets were clean and smelled of… I don't know. Violets?" And then, his voice lewd and low, "They'd been *ironed*, Lee, those sheets."

"Now this rain, did it…?"

"Yes! Exactly right. Warm rains!"

Lee also blushed. He was not so certain that he ought be listening to confessions of this particular cast, sweet ones that harkened back to the youth of the West. "And then what happened?"

"And then I was ten."

Lee, remembering his own history at that age, braced himself.

"Ten was I, yes, or maybe less, when one morning I awoke a little earlier than normal and found the dawn somewhat more beautiful than usual. And you must understand, Lee, that in those days the mornings were *far* superior to what now passes for the same."

"Before the youth of the West...?"

"Just so. Well! I couldn't lie abed in weather like that, certainly not, and never mind the sheets. Mile after mile, the world in perfect clarity, each rooftop its rooster and trees like corduroy upon the hills." He stopped. Already he had plucked half a bushel of grass, stuffing some of it into his pocket, some his pipe, and donating the rest to the breeze. "Ah, Lee, my glass is empty, and I have no wine."

The boy fetched it, his mind pondering darkly upon what he had heard. He had less than an hour before sunfall, and then, the Director would emerge from his dwelling and lock the gates. And even after squeezing through the bars, Lee would still be facing the long trek homeward with the danger of clowns lying in wait.

The bookmaster still sprawled in the yard, charmed, apparently, by two high-wheeling crows who had found a route into the valley, and now were tossing down a non-stop stream of sarcasms upon both man and boy.

"And then what happened?"

"Ah, Lee, I have very little left to tell you."

"I'm ready."

"But will you still come for visits, I wonder, bringing little gifts? No, I think you're one of those who watches and absorbs, and having done so, comes back no more!"

Lee tried to protest, but the man held up his hand to stop him.

"Twenty little shops you passed, stores and marts. Oh, Lee, I would have accepted almost anything, glass figurines, imported foods, anything that showed a proper tribute on the part of youth to the part of wisdom, and of me."

"Yes, sir. Well, I reckon I'd better get on back now. Heck, they're liable to lock the gates on me!" He laughed, riotously so, laughing alone.

"Leave, you say? But what about the toughs? No, no, you can sneak past them much more safely in full night. And besides, they'll be drunk by that time."

There was truth in that.

"Nor do they have your eye for trails and for the moon. So! Where were we?"

"The third time..."

"Third! Third and last; the rest of my life has mostly been waste. And someday, Lee, you'll be waste, too." He drank at length and then, smacking his lips over it, proceeded:

"You must remember, Lee, that I had been outside playing, playing hard, playing all day with sticks and..."

"We've already done that one."

"Oh? Oh, yes! Yes, the third happiness came when I was traveling at night in a car. Did I mention the radio had music on it? The fatal combination of a lantern in the woods viewed to the sound of chamber music?"

"Yes, sir. Lantern."

"And music, too, Lee. That's crucial."

"Yes, sir. Music."

"And night."

Lee nodded, at the same time glancing to the sky where, indeed, the gathering night seemed just about ready to leap down in great surprise upon an unexpecting world. "Night, yes, sir."

"Well, then, there you have it, my whole life. And now, I suppose, you won't be coming back anymore?"

"I might."

"No."

"I might."

"No. Philip won't, and now you won't, either. Ah, well, you'd best hurry, if you must. Those buzzards are behaving somewhat bolder than I like to see."

They shook with formality. Surely the man was too cultivated to regret any visits of his, or so Lee told himself as he departed down the lane. And then, too, the dark was falling fast. To Lee's mind, it resembled a gathering of particles, each swelling to enormous size until conjoined by others.

He hurried, waiting until he came to the crossroads before turning and waving at the man, who stood signaling with his handkerchief. And now, for courage, Lee took a cigarette and ignited it on his first attempt. For if he must be seen, then let him be seen like this — running home through danger in great jauntiness.

It was but a tiny village, archetypical for its time and place, if not indeed even more so than most such places. He ran past a two-hundred-year-old home, a narrow structure, very tall, whose manifold gables supported an owl here and a bat there and, atop the chimney, an agitated cat scratching at the moon. The reason Lee stopped to watch was because of the two-hundred-year-old woman who had come out onto her porch in order to enjoy the presumptively mild night with fireflies and cicadas and, having found none — Lee bowed sweepingly to her — had turned away sadly and gone back in.

Next came a yard fenced with palings, with some half-dozen grumbling hogs inside it, staring down in perfect discontent at the little bit of earth that their weak eyes in the increasing dark could still read. Very different were the dogs of the town, a more vigilant species by far, some of them coming out to the very edges of their properties to snap at Lee. And one dog in particular, a tawny male, three feet tall, was built for heroism. If Lee could add this dog to the horse he already owned, and add to both a wife (or a girlfriend at any rate), then his happiness would have been complete. Instead, he stopped for a moment beneath the street lamp and read a few pages, good ones.

The downtown district was abandoned, vacant, possibly extinct. He tiptoed past the bakery, looking neither into the window nor, when he came to it, into the tavern where more than once he had dreamt of being pulled inside and mistreated and left to drown in pools of beer. He especially refused to glance toward the jail and its prisoner who, for the first time in memory, was *not* singing one of his obscene songs. More interesting to Lee were the overhead apartments that housed the shopkeepers and their families, including several girls. Theirs was the privilege of rising on any given morning and looking down into the town itself, where things were more interesting than anywhere else in the county and where — and this was the part Lee liked –they could do it without themselves ever being seen at all! Thinking of it, he began to hum, but then soon fell silent again when he acknowledged how ill that puerile behavior sorted with his cigarette and the publications in his vest.

He traveled five blocks, smoking (always smoking), humming (humming unconsciously), and continually thinking at very high speed. Tonight, around each lamppost, the bats were blue and glossy and excessively plump from too many easy feasts upon moths as gregarious as these. Unfortunately, he had also been talking to himself, as he belatedly realized when he spotted a woman watching with concern from her second-story apartment — concern that he was speaking and concern that it was into her neighborhood that he had chosen to come. The truth was that he had read too many books, had Lee, already he had. Not that he had waxed plump from it! On the contrary. And *never* glossy.

He passed into the rich zone: five rich houses holding their noses at him. Here, the dogs were sentient to an extreme degree and entertained nothing but contempt for boys like Lee. Remarkably, this was followed by the most impoverished of districts. In fact, he found it lovely here, lovely poverty, more interesting by far than mere extravagence. But even more interesting than that was one particular shack painted a shade of green that had weathered down to a hue of turquoise, applied over what looked like driftwood; he needed only to blow upon it in order to push it over. He knew, of course, that he was being evaluated by some dozen or more eyes watching from the darkened porch across the road. Came now a hound shaking his jowls at him. Lee decided to leave.

Two blocks further, he acquired a sidereal view of "Mahler's Head," a ravaged formation in which the mile-high genius seemed particularly troubled. Harkening to it, Lee thought that he could hear faraway horns calling from the hills. "Debussy" and "Ravel," he could see them, too, one slightly broader than the other who, however, was perhaps somewhat the taller. Yes, certainly he realized that the farm people had very different names for them — "Shoat Bottom," for example, and "Blister Hill." Lee snorted. Slowly and slowly he was losing all patience with this class of people, a stunted race who cared nothing for the distinction between hog snouts and human genius. He had to stop and remind himself that it was the ancestors of these same people who, in old times, had given the highest of the hills the name of "KÔ-WE-TÄN-AMI," or "It Blackens Out The Sun."

He arrived at the church and the queer little cemetery with its two score of gravestones picturing scenes from the lives and professions of the deceased. One man had been a baker while his brother, who had died young, was seen removing the actual loaves with a long-handle ladle shaped like a spade. It did surprise Lee to find one stone, in Hittite apparently, that portrayed what appeared to be an ancient battle scene with some very furious elephants and, in the corner of the inscription, a pile of penis-trophies taken from the slain. But what most affected him was one certain tablet where the engraver had started out with enthusiasm but then, like an author with nothing in his head, had put down his chisel and gone away.

Danger came on the outskirts of town, where two clowns of his own general size were loitering next to the soft drink machine. Lee, putting on a rugged expression, moved forward, observing at the same time that one of the clowns, probably drunk, was wearing a false plastic nose held in place with a string. It was the other boy who first set eyes on Lee.

"Hey! C'mere a minute, shithead."

Lee slowed. He might, or might not, have to take a beating. What he knew he must never do is run away from fools. And then, too, he was only slightly shorter in height and lighter in heaviness than the average of those two, once those two were added by size and weight and divided by their numbers.

"Where you going, shithead? Back to the 'Cademy?"

"Yeah! So's he can *study*."

"Thinks he's too good for us. Don't you?"

"Little bit," said Lee.

"Wha…!"

"But wait! I didn't used to be."

"Son-of-a-bitch! Son-of-a-*bitch*! You hear what he said?"

"I heard him. Alright, what makes you so fucking good then — that's what I want to know."

Lee pointed to his brain, but then changed his mind and pointed instead to his heart. Changing again, he pointed to that part where, according to Galen, the Will was lodged.

"*Son-of-a-bitch*! See what he's doing there, pointing?"

"I seen him. OK, so tell me this, then, if you're so fucking smart!"

Lee waited for the question, which, however, never came.

"Why, you ain't big enough to…"

"Naw, I don't need to be big. Just smart."

"Son-of-a-bitch! Did you hear…?"

"I heard him. OK, tell me this, then, how'd you get to be so fucking smart?" Suddenly he held up his hand. "Now I'm not saying you *are* smart, you understand."

Lee looked at them. He could have smote one boy with the Lucretius and the other with the poetry; the books were thick enough and he had hands for both. Instead, he said:

"Actually, you're just too flagitious to understand what I'm talking about."

The word appeared to stun them. Five seconds went by slowly, giving Lee the most extreme pleasure. Generous to a fault, he added then:

"Naw, it's not your fault."

"Son-of-a...! Somebody ought to shoot you, you know that?"

It was too late, however, to shoot him — already a man had come from the store, the father of the one with the nose, to judge from his wide suspenders and the cud of tobacco that he was working over in his mouth. Lee waited as the three of them climbed into the wagon, whipped up the mule and then, with the two boys peering back painfully through dust and murk, drove away.

Lee still had awaiting him a two-mile run through hideous woods. Far away, in the direction of Tennessee, a radio tower had gone into a panic, its once-golden lamp now throwing out urgent signals that assailed the South. Availing himself of that meager light, Lee was bemused to come upon an opossum, the world's stupidest who, trusting to fortune, was dangling in full open view. Bears once had abided in these forests, before the hill barbarians had massacred all of them for their claws and kidneys.

Usually, nothing surprised Lee anymore, not until he came back to the Academy grounds and, after throwing himself across the boundary, discovered a cohort of gammas splitting firewood by the light of the stars. Lee nodded to the reeve, a prudent man who kept well out of range of the boys who, after all, were armed with axes and lengths of wood. Lee now stepped forward into the light and began to probe disdainfully with his left slipper among the four or five taking an undeserved rest. How they loathed him, those who had refused to do their Greek? Lee smiled. But what new, strange pleasure, pray — being widely abhorred — was this? To test it, he went back and did it again, strolling and probing and barely troubling to acknowledge the overseer who tipped his hat three times before finally coming to realize that, in Lee's presence, he really ought to stand.

The last hundred yards were by far the most perilous. Satisfying himself that he was not being followed, he burst around the corner and into the settlement proper, veering away at the last instant before crashing into the lake. Broaching up to the window, he saw that Young Edmund was at his desk, he who used to be such a whimperer, and was conversing with himself happily in his narrow cell. Four other lights could also be seen — Goldman's, the gardener's, and the glow that came from the apartment where dwelt the boy who was deemed the best of them all. Peeping in upon him, Lee began gnashing his teeth. He hated to share the world with someone who, week after week and pound for pound, might be superior to himself — it was an agony, a thistle in the blood and a scorpion in the soul, nor could he have counted the tears it had cost him. He prayed that the boy might die abominably and soon and in great pain, before he came to full power.

By midnight Lee had achieved all his tasks, had polished his teeth, gotten into his bedclothes and turned down the covers in his fastidious way. This would be the moment to script his dream for the oncoming night and then... No. First he must get into bed.

Three times longer than it needed to be, his cot was narrow and thin and in great part responsible, no doubt, for what his future physique would finally turn out to be. He did like to sleep in it, an exercise he carried out to perfection with his two hands pasted at his side, thumbs up, eyes forward. In this way, if he should die while still unconscious, Goldman would find him pre-prepared for burial, a tiny ceremony to be carried out at sundown on Mahler's Nose.

He dreamt that he was traveling by night in a car along a country road with a silo here and a barn there, and withal fields of indigo on both sides. Apparently he was not to be privileged to pick up the sound of crickets and cicadas whose cries, for some reason, had not passed over into the dream state. Still, he was quite content. Was anyone sitting next to him in the Packard? He believed so, and believed also that it was his own future wife whom, however, he was not yet entitled to gaze upon.

He traveled far, sometimes sleeping and sometimes not. It startled him to come upon a scarecrow or, sometimes, a confused person in tattered apparel standing precisely in the center of a thirty-acre field. Then came the most unsettling part of all, a fully unclothed woman — until Lee recognized her as simply an intrusion from last Tuesday's dream.

When, toward three in the morning, he narrowed in upon a certain farmhouse, two stories tall, he turned at once and aimed for it. He was always able to recognize it after long absences, with someone glowing in the door, a glimpse of furniture inside and a dog on the porch. It was here that his friends and family had gathered, all of them waving kerchiefs and cheering him across the last few inches. Not that he'd ever actually reach them, of course. No, he understood well enough that, for him, the age of friends and family was over, and that for such as he had become, there was to be no journey like that. For it was only in dreams alone that he had not already lost the knack for it, of friends, family, and farm.

Fifteen

Through the curling flower places he could see Philip, and through those same places the other boy could see Lee. It was Lee's best of days when, as a result of the previous month's hard work in paleontology and Greek, he was privileged to sit off by himself at a table of his own, there to be waited upon by his own special boy, a small one called Burt. Thus Lee comported himself—three times he shifted this way and that, arranging himself in such a way so that Philip could not fail to see who it was who was now sitting in the chair to which he had been accustomed.

A thousand years might go by before Lee was again given Table Number One at mess. Or maybe not, provided that his brain cells continued to go on fattening and splitting, a headache-producing process that made him question whether the organ might not actually burst out through the seams and keep on growing, running past the sun. Accordingly, Lee now reached up as if to organize his hair, but in actuality to verify the size of his unending head.

He liked to eat his beans with cigarettes and wine and then, still humming, liked to slice up his small portion of meat (which only he and Goldman had been given) into standard geometric shapes that could be fitted together to form more complicated things. Had Philip seen that? Had he seen how the Director and he had nodded to each other in cordial fashion across the darkened room? Suddenly Lee took up his heavy iron fork and began beating chimes on his ice-filled tumbler, whereupon Burt ran immediately to his side.

"Now, Burt," Lee said, "I want you to fetch me some of that rhubarb pie."

The boy wrote it down.

"With cheese on it."

"Right. Cheese."

"Now Burt… Do you mark me?"

"Sure! I do."

"Then tell Mrs. Arnsdorf that I do wish she'd move this way a few inches. I can't hear the cello with her sitting behind that column."

The boy dashed off, slowed, stopped, and then came back.

"What should I do first, Lee? The cello, or…?"

"Pie, Burt. Pie."

Thus was Burt.

When, just after twilight, the repast moved into its final stages, Goldman sneezed twice and then, after struggling with his chair and napkin, managed to rise and stay there. There were but seventeen persons in that room and his voice was able to reach each one of them.

"Gentlemen," he said, "you have done well, some of you."

Silence followed. Lee thought at first that he was preparing to sit again; instead, after wheezing noisily two or three times, hoisting his trousers and drinking more ice water from his enormous goblet, he went on:

"Gentlemen! It was never my intention to make you miserable, never. Or, anyway, not for its own sake alone, absolutely not. Oh, yes, to be sure, a certain degree of misery is perhaps necessary before one can break through into those *higher* miseries that… I'm digressing. But look at Young Edmund Burchem! *He's* not miserable. Are you, Edmund? Stand up, boy, so we can see you."

Edmund stood, all eyes turning in his direction and verifying there was no misery there whatsoever. In fact, the boy was grinning.

"Edmund, Edmund, Edmund, youngest of our scholars. And someday, Ed, you'll be sitting there where Lee is sitting — provided he doesn't steal the chair."

Lee grinned. It was a fairly good moment for him; all eyes were his and Arnsdorf's woman had, in the meantime, begun to play the concerto that was a particular favorite with him at that time. Goldman said:

"And so let's praise you all. Stand, Philip, so's we can see you. I had a golden trophy for you, boy, but I seem to have left it at home. Sit, sit, we know what you look like. Now! Are you ready for the news?"

There was general and wide-spread assent, each boy and every scholar of them agreeing that they were prepared for good news in any amount that Goldman could deliver.

"Very well. Tonight, my friends, we celebrate — that's right! — celebrate our achievements. *Your* achievements, I mean. Me, I don't achieve. No, I just… I'm straying."

"'Celebrate,' you said."

"Yes!"

Lee ran back in a panic to his apartment, delighted and alarmed, horrified and charmed to know that, within an hour, he was to attend his first "party" in two years. Of clothes, he had only a few in his closet, fewer still on his person, and even less than that in the crate where he kept his chess set and stamp collection. Even so, he did manage to put together, not a suit precisely, but an ensemble of a shirt, cloak, and trousers along with footwear, two books, and a splash of cologne. Dressed thus, he burst from his suite and was running at high speed toward the oratory when, seeing that Burt was running too, he slowed precipitously and began to move forward in a much more deliberate and stately fashion.

He had expected to come into a room decorated with bunting, a fire going, and cider and apples percolating in the kettle; instead, seeing what he saw, he jumped back in horror and amazement of the most extreme kind. The bunting was there, more indeed than he had planned upon. Good things to eat—he could see those, too -- cakes and the like set out upon a long, narrow table that extended far into the distance. Arnsdorf was there—Lee had been sure that he would be—and his wife as well, one of them armed with a cello and the other, the man, making a small repair to his violin. Philip was there. Edmund, of course. Spivey. Lee therefore ought to have felt entirely at home, save only for the presence of a small number of…

Girls. He reeled and then, reaching for something to hold onto, needed five full seconds before he could climb back into his bored expression. Plain, common whores, they seemed to him. Or, anyway, he saw one who was, or soon was to become, plain and common, and probably would become a whore as well, judging from her earrings and lipstick. Edging down along the wall, Lee kept well clear of her. He far preferred the others, nice girls all. But mostly he preferred the little black-headed exhibit who had taken her punch and cookies and had gone off by herself to examine certain of Philip's drawings, plain, common rubbish that had been tacked up along one side of the foyer. He considered offering her a cigarette and might have done so, had he not then detected in her a certain facial expression that stayed only briefly, though not so briefly that he couldn't see that she was not for him.

He went on, squeezing between Burchem and that other boy, who was said to be the best of them all, whose look of boredom was, perhaps, unfeigned. Goldman, in the meantime, had waddled out into the middle of the room where he was in the best of all locations for observing the social "chemistry" now taking place on all sides; Lee could see him rubbing his hands, chuckling, sometimes lifting up his little toy telescope and peering with it into the numerous corners of the octagonal room. And yet they had not been there five minutes before Young Edmund was dancing with the whore.

Lee sat. The room was dim, certainly, but not so much so that he couldn't read. Furthermore, he had already done all the dancing that he was ever likely to do, having finished with all that by the time he was twelve. And then, too, he couldn't feature himself dancing to the up-tempo version of Shostakovich on offer from the Arnsdorfs. And that, of course, was when a little brown-headed girl came and threw herself down in the adjoining chair.

"Hi!" she said.

Lee nodded.

"I think it's so good," she said, "what y'all are doing. Mr. Goldman, I mean."

Lee agreed. "What's he doing?"

"Bible school! And it's good for the local economy, too. My daddy said so."

Lee frowned. Already he had decided not to offer this one a cigarette. She had no bosoms, of course, nothing like that, nor did he expect any such things upon a girl whose mouth was full of "daddy" and the Bible.

"I've got my own horse," he said in tired voice, "and sometimes we go all the way up to Mah... Snout Hill. Also, I can swim for a hundred yards."

"Me, too."

"Underwater?"

"Oh."

He put on a bored expression. Goldman was watching, and Lee was beginning to experience a great wish to be done with this particular girl. A minute went by. Then:

"What are you reading? Must be good."

In fact, the book was only moderately good. Lee turned forward to that place where a series of illustrations showed some of the actual pottery that dated back to the period discussed. This whole book had been written, not by any single man alone, but a slew of them; bearded men, many of them, ethnologists, archeologists and people of that kind—their joint photograph appeared on page 212. Putting aside his cigarette, Lee now referred back to the opening paragraph, which had promised so much. He realized that Philip, not thirty feet away, was watching everything he did.

That boy had brought a book of his own, heavier than Lee's. Seated thus and dressed in his paper hat, its rubber band running under his chin, a cookie in one hand and wine in the other, a foot-long noise-maker dead in his mouth, and two girls crowding him on the left... They glared at each other. It revealed bad taste, Lee believed, that the boy, ordinarily so calm, would allow his chagrin for someone else sitting at Table Number One to be as obvious as obviously it was, all of which rendered Lee very happy, indeed. "Soon," Lee said, speaking to himself, "I shall sit there always. And what can you do about it, hm? Nothing, nothing, nothing." *This* was the message he now signaled to Philip, who blinked once and then pretended he had some sudden, good reason to turn and look away. Nothing, nothing, nothing and never, never, never had anyone ever been able to stand up under *Lee's* gaze. Next, he tried out that gaze on Spivey who, however, was too excited by the social interactions going on about him to stop and look back. Instead, the man smiled, waved, drank, and then suddenly leapt up in gentlemanly fashion to offer his chair to one of the guests.

"I'm Ada," said the girl seated next to Lee. "That's what they call me, but my real name is Adalgisa."

Never, never, never had Lee been able to use his Will on Goldman—the man was simply too phlegmatic and large for that. Thinking of it, he fell into a depression of sorts, despite Philip's bad mood. Burchem, meanwhile, appeared to have traded his girl for another who, although by far the prettiest in the whole group, was much too tall for the boy. They danced well, however. Breasts, if she had any, would be pressing just now into Young Edmund's face. At the same time, the whore had gone off by herself, where she was pretending to have an interest—Lee knew what she was really interested in—in the collection of birds' eggs that Philip had set up in a glass case that also held a few artifacts from Choctaw days.

It was near to eight o'clock at night before Lee finally admitted to himself that he simply did not wish to continue any further with this particular book. What, really, had he to do with these blue, boring speculations on tribal organization? Let all organizations be organized like this one — with Edmund here and Philip there and Lee not speaking to either of them. Thinking of it, he took two cigarettes and handed one to 'Gisa, who put it in her purse.

"Want to dance?" he asked. "I don't."

"Sure!"

"Anyway, I've been developing too fast."

Spivey was dancing with the geologist's wife, a woman who was so old and fragile that the librarian soon parked her at the refreshment table, and then went to look at Philip's displays. Lee's spirits now darkened even further, to be lifted only slightly when he heard his horse striving to communicate with him from half a mile away, down the path and across the lake.

"And *now* what are you thinking?"

Lee shrugged. He had no wish to burden this girl, who had never done harm to him, with his over-developed ideas. "Oh, I don't know," he said. "Philosophy, stuff like that."

She came nearer, trying to see into his eye. Adalgisa she may well be, even if to him she looked like a girl from one of the nearby farms.

"What kind of…philosophy?"

"Want some punch?"

Far away, his horse neighed again. Lee turned at the sound, catching Philip "out of position" as it were, which is to say wearing an expression that revealed more about the boy's underlying unhappiness than the boy himself would have wanted to be seen. Could Lee still thrash this boy after so many weeks of hard study and too much reading? Easily. But could he still thrash the both of them together, Philip and Young Burchem? No. No, those two would *never* have agreed to cooperate on any such endeavor. Could he have thrashed any of the adult men? In truth, probably not, or anyway not without a weapon. Could Lee, with redoubled effort, read all the books in Spivey's keeping? He could not.

By 9:45, Lee had excused himself and had wandered on down to the lake's edge, where he could more easily pick up sounds coming from the stable. Shielding his eyes, he scanned for swans and ducks and, finally, coming down to within an inch of the surface and stretching wide his eye (and bringing his Will into play), strove to see what the trout were doing at this hour. This proved a mistake; he could see nothing but the reflection of the stars and moon, all of which appeared six times larger than they should. Drunk, was he? Drunk on punch, too much reading, Adalgisa? Bending further over the water, he attempted to inspected at close range his favorite planet, whose rugged inspect terrain had always… And that, of course, was when one of the trout came up, snatched the star from under his eye and ran away with it!

There were other stars, other trout and, from the oratory, other music coming from Arnsdorf's tireless arm. Lee stayed where he was, giving his Will a rest. He made no further effort to go on reading. Rather, a sort of sadness came down over him when he saw how, for his benefit alone, the lake had changed into a veritable *camera obscura* that immediately began to throw off pictures of far-away parts of the world. He saw North Carolina and, nearer at hand, Spivey dancing with 'Gisa. But now Lee understood that he had extended himself about as far as he could, lest he wished to end up drowning in the stuff.

Sixteen

A fine thing, that Greek was held as early as it was. It allowed Lee to analyze at leisure the rosy-fingered dawn that sorted so well with certain poetic passages of great importance in the text. And then, when Greek was over, oftentimes he used to hurry back to his suite to regroup and close the doors. No one came here anymore, not unless they did it in his absence. Nor could they come then, not without leaving evidence of it in the form of a book out of kilter or footprints in the dust. And if he were fastidious to an extreme degree, yet he was also unsanitary to a fault. Dust, in short, meant nothing to him, not so long as his belongings remained in rational order. And that was when he recollected something that had come down to him through Goldman, namely that, whereas he might now and again experience some little bit of loneliness, soon he would lose all capacity for emotions of that kind.

Lee had not — not yet — apportioned his book stock into the three branches of world knowledge. His third room, the one nearest to the lake, contained his cot, his fishing equipment, and not much else. (There was still an incumbent in room number four, although Lee had reason to hope for his impending removal.) It was owing to this that Lee had concentrated the best part of his library in his original quarters — the space was big enough and had good shelving in it, and never had the ceiling been known to leak, no matter what rains came into the valley. Here, waking two or three times during the course of a night and taking his flashlight, he could ascertain at a glance that, first, nothing was missing and then, secondly, that certain passages of high importance remained within the texts.

He liked to take down two books and lay them flat. After opening one of them, suddenly he would open the other, too. Or, he liked to take a title from the topmost shelf and then open it at random and read at hazard. Soon, he would find himself deep into something that had occurred, for example, in the Thirteenth or even the Fourteenth century, and with the promise of good reading all the way to the Fifteenth before Alabama's somewhat histrionic sun would leap up, each day a little earlier, and put a stop to it.

After that, he could not go on reading. Nor did he understand how books had come to be written, nor history enacted, not as long as life was subject to the mandates of a sun that, even as he glared at it, appeared to be composed primarily of worms. Unwilling to return to bed, he would make up his cot to perfection, spending a long time on it, and after preparing a new pot of coffee, would dress himself slowly in his shirt, cloak, sandals, and pantaloons. Generally, he had no particular interest in what he wore; he did, however, cherish his cape, a crimson swatch of velveteen stitched by Mrs. Arnsdorf with his own personal motto in golden thread. This garment he now unfolded with care and then held aloft for the dawn to read, assuming as he did that, here, the dawns were good at reading French.

He liked to come into town at high speed, appearing instantaneously where he was least expected. One single dog came out to greet him, a self-effacing sort of personality who had come to rely upon Lee, and Lee alone, for his weekly ration of pats and conversation.

Next came the bakery, his favorite location in the state. He liked to represent himself as a starveling, as it were, and stand there with his eyes fixed upon a freshly-baked loaf until the proprietor weakened or a woman came along. But not now, not today; it was too early for women and too early for alms, and too early by much for consuming such stuff as new-made loaves. He therefore continued on to the hardware store.

It was too early here, too. Pressing against the window, he thought that he could discern the storekeeper deep within, a squat man, very serious about tools and bolts and baling wire, who was stirring about in his private quarters that sufficed also as an upholstery shop. He could see the man's wife, too, a person who covered her face each night — Lee was accustomed to this by now — covered it with a thick white paste of some kind. Lee pressed nearer. No one had to know that he was using the window as yet one more *camera obscura*, his latest bad habit, and that this in turn let him see more than he should. And what he saw just now was the reflection of the milkman on the other side of the road, a worried-looking personality in a humiliating uniform. Lee followed him, waiting patiently each time until the man had deposited a jar of contracted milk or cream on some porch or doorstep.

Thus Lee spent the morning, running here and running there and keeping one eye at all times upon the steeple. Very soon now at the bell, sending the pigeons into flight. Accordingly, Lee now raced for the tower and the iron ladder that offered a pathway to the sky. Halfway to the top, he left his emptied milk bottle on one of the struts and kept on climbing. This was where he had always wanted to be, in the final moment before history's last instant—dangling by one hand while going through his morning crafts, Greek verbs, *miles* above the town.

Seventeen

The following day, he saddled his steed and called to him by his new name, a six-syllable title taken from a piece of devotional literature that had recently come across his desk. They were doing well, the horse and Lee, both of them driving repeatedly into the lake's icy surf and reveling in it. It caused Lee to turn his gaze toward that high-soaring salient of basalt known in the community as Mahler's Tongue. Hypnotized by how it sparkled, there where the gland protruded to its utmost extent, as if the mile-high genius had been lapping at the dew, Lee did not at first observe the drove of gammas being prodded to the field by the wrangler and the overseer. For one, brief moment, Lee almost weakened, seeing the state they were in. But as for the bullet-headed boy, he, at least, was no more to be seen among them, not since his funeral last week. Dead of glanders, the boy had perished from his long—indeed, perhaps over-long—assignment to the stables. "But don't *you* worry," Arnsdorf had said to Lee. "Bovines can't get it."

To the east and west, there were other hills than those named after composers. Springing aboard his mount, Lee now piloted toward a series of blunt piles, expired volcanoes bearing the names of some of the better-documented Fourth-century Egyptian anchorites. After a moderately hard climb, the horse and he ought to be able to look down into all that southern part of the county that someday would be named after... Must it be Philip? Couldn't it be Lee?

He had not progressed very far before he dashed into that self-same, unperturbed, and above-mentioned *Philip* who, today, was bringing his well-attested little knapsack, a frayed article on which Mrs. Arnsdorf had emblazoned the most breathtakingly arrogant motto to have been adopted by any of the boys. Fired-up by the botany master, and praised to the skies, the knave was going from flower to flower, distraining the poor things of their seeds and petals, and sometimes even their private stamens. Not that there was any shortage of such things! Not on Buffon Knoll. Lee followed at a distance, smirking at the boy's hobby. Suddenly, he spun about, surprised and displeased to find that Young Edmund was following *him*.

Indeed, it appeared, on this spring day, as if the entire institution had come pouring out of doors in order to get a closer look at things and try out the various hillside pathways. Lee, too, had been advancing at such an alarming rate these last weeks that when he opened his mouth to speak, as he did now, the words were inclined to tumble out in a jumble of disorganized lines of which some was real poetry, some Greek, some came from magazines and some, too much really, was pure rubbish left over from radio stories.

He drove higher, halting again when he came to an open view of the egregious Birmingham, "rectum of the South," as Arnsdorf called it. However, it was *their* world, *their* city, and *their* modality, as the man had gone on to say. Suddenly, the horse and Lee leapt back two spaces, the result of a muffled explosion telling where one of the steel mills had exploded. He knew well the attachment of people to their jobs and cars and their appalling habit of coming together within tight confines called "cities," there to depend upon one another and — and here Lee snorted out loud — to satisfy certain human *needs*. Just to think about it made him want to puke. He spun about and threw a hard look at Edmund, sending the boy off in another direction.

Toward noon, with a mountain on one side and another on the other, he began to ascend the slope known for obvious reasons as HARB-JU-JO-RUM. And, if at one time it had been a perfect formation, symmetrical and full of grace, now the whole upper structure had "slipped," as the clowns of the district said, to end up at Mahler's feet. Here, for the first time, the horse began to demur, hesitant to take on a climb as arduous as that. Lee nevertheless persisted in urging him forward, finally taking out one of the little sugar cubes which the animal dearly loved, and allowing him to see it.

Never would Lee have expected to find the music master and his wife at this elevation. He stopped and recoiled, forcing the horse to backtrack into the pines, where almost the first thing he noted was another of the sacred bowers, built in old times by the original people called "Croatoans." Dismounting, he went to inspect the basin and pestle, both stained with the darkened residue of sacrificial blackberries and aloe leaves. Next, he began slowly and noiselessly to creep forward to spy upon the professor and his wife.

They had brought a blanket with them, a basket of food and several books, and with this equipment had ascended to levels that Lee assumed only students could reach. Moving with circumspect — the weeds were tall but also far apart — he crawled nearer. That these two were actually interacting with each other, as it were, which is to say lying side by side and feeding deeply into one another's eyes... At first Lee was disgusted with them. But then, as he inched his way to a better view, his opinion grew somewhat better, too. It was their affair, none of his, nor could he posit a single reason why fat people should not also be in love. He watched, entranced, as the woman pulled a bloom from the bed of yellow flowers they were lying in, and began to tease her husband with it, tickling him among his nose and warts. That these two people, in spite of everything, in spite of the West and its current condition, in spite of warts and being overweight, that they could find it in themselves to cavort like that... Lee drew back. He would need to think more deeply about this later on.

Lee, too, was dallying, not with any woman of course, but with early spring. And now, with the sun faltering and the stars hurrying into position, Philip trudging homeward and owls blaring, the cicadas chiming up and the sun coming back for a last respite, *this* was the moment that Lee had set aside for galloping across the wold. But he got no further than the weald when he leapt back for the third time that day, amazed to see that Philip had turned off his path and taken a seat in the chair-shaped boulder that looked out over the institution, a piece of furniture that Lee had always thought belonged to himself alone. He sometimes questioned whether he had ever done or thought anything that Philip had not already thought or done before him. At once, Lee drove around to the other side. Nothing surprised him anymore — it never had — and yet what he saw now surprised him greatly. The brilliant boy had thrown his specimens away and now sat curled into a ball, swaying back and forth while weeping the most bitter and heartfelt tears that Lee had ever witnessed. For one, brief moment, Lee thought of coming forward, of helping the boy gather his petals and other things and allowing him to ride on the horse. No. Instead, Lee withdrew. He must think about this more deeply later on.

The sun, now altogether dissolute, was pouring off in streams of sand. Lee was looking forward to a successful descent and then a good, hot meal at Table Number Three or, if his work had merited it, Table Number Two in the order of the mess; instead, at that moment, he recognized that he had inadvertently fallen into step with one of the peasants traveling the same trail. But whereas Leland had a horse at the end of his string, the peasant, a lanky, grinning, whey-eyed type who deserved the title of "clown" better than any that Lee had met so far, his string was attached only to a lamb. For some moments, they marched side-by-side, neither speaking. At the same time, Lee's cloak was wafting out behind him in the breeze, the way he liked it. The other man was wearing bib overalls with a missing strap.

"Howdy."

"Yes, sir; good day for it, walking."

"Sun's going down."

"It might. Rained, they say, over to Calauria County."

"Nothing surprises me anymore."

"Sun's down."

"Could rain here, too."

"I suppose. Now, just what in the hell kind of thing is that you're wearing there, boy? V-I-V-R-A-I T-O-U-J-O-U-R-S? I bet that's something real snotty, am I right?"

Lee held out his hand, palm up, feeling no rain of any sort. "Had better than an inch, they say, in Wetumpka."

They continued on, moving somewhat slower than Lee would have preferred. He discerned the path that would have carried him home, saw it come up and then fall behind, all because he was too courteous to break off a conversation, even with a clown.

"Little son-of-a-bitch goes to that there 'Cademy—that's what I said. Was I right about that?"

Lee admitted that he was.

"Lots of strange things going on down there. That what they say."

"We could use a little rain, actually. The farmers could."

"Goddamn bunch of crazy people is what it is! I don't know, I just don't see why a feller like you with a horse like him, why you'd want to get mixed up with folks like that, I just don't. Shit, I seen one of 'em down at the Post Office a couple days ago—big ole fat man."

"He's not so bad."

"I wouldn't say that. You et yet?"

"Yesterday."

"Yester…! Hell, boy, I'm talking *today*!" He pointed toward his cabin, an adorable little structure with turfen roof, a hammock on the porch, and a significant pile of firewood out back. As for the wood, Lee could start in right away and still it would have required him half a month to put it into an order in which all the sticks would lie in parallel. "'Course now, if you're too grand for the likes of us…"

"Heck, no!" said Lee. "Shoot, I live in the country, too. Or used to. Or rather…"

"Used to be one of us. Now you're one of them."

"A little bit."

"Shit, boy, they done *ruint* you!"

The cabin was low, dark, full of smoke, the invariable southern hound with missing tail snoozing precisely in the center of the earthen floor. Becoming aware of a stranger in their midst, the animal opened first one eye and then the next, and began to analyze Lee's underlying nature.

"He won't hurt you."

"I know."

"What do you mean you 'know?' He *might* hurt you."

"Naw, I've had lots worse dogs than him."

"Oh."

They proceeded forward, winding their way through a bedroom that smelled of camphor and ashes, linseed and lavender, and thence into the parlor where sat the man's mother or, mayhap, grandmother indeed. Over and over, these words ran through Lee's mind: "Yes, it's me, having another adventure. Three in one week!"

"Mama, this here's… Hell, I don't even know your name!"

Lee gave it, a noble one taken from his recent work in Greek.

"Hector ain't had nothing to eat since yesterday."

"Lands!" She rose painfully — Lee saw that she been thumbing through an album of old photographs — and fixed the shawl about her shoulders. "I reckon I could offer him some of those collards."

"With black-eyed peas and pot gravy? Yes, ma'am."

"Hector used to be like us, mama; that's why he *loves* those peas. Ain't that right?"

Lee grinned. They were ignorant. He experienced a huge tenderness just now for all such people everywhere, collard-eaters whose wealth — nine jars of golden plum jelly — had been set out for maximum visibility on the second shelf of the china cabinet. Between the stove and jelly, the dog and photo album, Lee could feel his whole philosophy teetering in the balance. Even now, it might not be too late for him, so much did the woman remind him of his own dear, dead grandmother.

"Yes," she said, "we're all the same. But I'll wager she didn't have as many hen pecks as me." She stretched out her hands, bony things larger than a man's. He counted there a very great many scars, indeed, including at least one place where the bird seemed actually to have broken the vein.

"Whew!" He pointed at the blackened vein.

"'Possum."

"Ma'am?"

"I figured he was dead. They do that, don't you know." Already she had taken out all manner of collards and peas, including the remains of a pork pie with a whole ear in it. Lee observed, but did not ask for, a gracefully-articulated decanter full of scuppernong wine. Even so, he found it disconcerting that they allowed the cat to sup off the same table with them. He therefore turned to the works of art—an etching of the Christ and, side by side with him, a certain famous football coach. Lee had hoped to eat in peace; instead:

"You don't got any business down there."

"Ma'am?"

"Down there. Why, you ain't nothing in this world but trash like us."

"I used to be."

"Still is! Why, Lord, that dog would of torn you to pieces! No, I seen what you are, soon as you walked in I seen it. 'Why, he ain't nothing in this world,' I said. Talking to myself, you understand. 'Why, he ain't nothing in this world but trash like us.'"

Lee nodded. He wanted to finish this meal.

"Ears sticking out. Look at 'em, Willard."

The meal had been good, his best in ages, and now, with the woman having gone back to her album, he was free to roam at large throughout the shack. Outside it was full dark, one small owl blaring in tedious repertoire. But *inside*, meanwhile, a police drama was coming in over the radio along with the sound of pistol shots and the cry of thugs. Harkening to it with one ear, Lee probed into the pantry, finding all manner of things in wonderful storage. It smelled of ginger in here, and gingerly did Lee smell of it. He uncovered a bottle of red pennies that had tarried so long in these aromatic precincts that a moss had germinated on the coins. Half-cent pieces, were they, those that had migrated to the bottom of the heap? He thought not, no. For although they were big enough and old, yet they did not have that unmistakable profile engraved on them, nor the horrible thinness that had characterized the authentic zinc half-penny Confederate discs that he remembered from his grandfather's closet, no. It didn't seem so awful to take just one while leaving behind a silver dime in an exchange that was more than fair.

He proceeded on to the sleeping quarters and a more in-depth observation of the bed coverings—true quilts, some of them, decorated with zodiacal signs, farm animals, and episodes from the Book of Daniel. He had always had a special liking for bedsteads that came supplied, like this bedstead, with a little three-level staircase that led up to a mellow mattress full of shucks and duck feathers and covered with taut sheets. His immediate compulsion was to ascend that abbreviated flight of steps and give the whole apparatus his most searching test. And then, nine hours later, his next impulse would have been to awaken in a mint-new day, much refreshed, with coffee, bacon and biscuits and, if he had his way, a compartmentalized serving dish with his three favorite kinds of jams and jellies. Thinking of it, he drifted into the second room, a far more barren sort of place with tools on the bedside table, no art anywhere, and individual shoes scattered here and there. Hurriedly, Lee managed to put them into general order even while detesting to touch the things. No art, no books, and the bed itself was so poorly made-up that Lee could see where some of the straw was coming out.

And yet the place did have a kerosene lamp in it. He ran toward it, finding the wick intact, the odor as it should be, and the mantle so perfectly coated in soot that he could have scratched his own personal motto in it. And did so.

Of libraries, they maintained only the most rudimentary kind—four volumes, apart from photograph albums, together with a Walter Scott and a badly dog-eared copy of the *Principia* of Whitehead and Russell. He read a small selection from it, and then, in danger of getting bored, sauntered out into the backyard where, for the past half-hour, the lout had been drinking steadily within the shelter of his muscadine arbor. This was *his* place, Lee understood, and no one else's; accordingly, he thought it best to be invited before he stepped inside.

"Want a pipe?"

"Naw, I'm only fourteen."

"Fourteen, shit. Shit, when I was fourteen I'd already been to Birmingham."

"I've been to Birmingham."

"To see a whore? Shit, when I was your age, shit, I was already making my own brew. How many deer you killed, boy?"

"I don't hold with killing 'em."

"Don't?"

"Naw. It's the eyes."

"God a'mighty, they done *ruint* you!"

The man, as Lee had already noticed, was continually chewing on a cud of some kind which he kept removing and immersing in his beverage. In short, he was smoking, chewing, scratching, and drinking, and never for one moment confusing any of the four. The more he drank and scratched, the more violent his discourse grew.

"Flatlanders! Goddamn eleemosynary trash!" And then, his voice dark and low, "'*Clowns*,' we call 'em. But I wouldn't want them to know that."

"No, no."

"I just might have to put a knife into that fat one."

"Naw. He ain't so bad."

"Now, just who in the goddamn hell do he think he am? Ex-quarterback or something?"

Lee remained silent. There *could* be a knifing; he knew these people and knew what they could do. "Wal," he said finally, for he had fallen back into his country speech, "reckon I'd better head on back."

"Sit down, Hector, you ain't going nowhere. And how come you're hanging around way over there in them shadows, like? I don't like that. Want some brew?"

"Naw, I'm only..."

"Fourteen. Shit, boy!"

"Besides, I got to get fifty more pages done tonight."

"What's that? What did you say just now?"

"Fifty."

"Shit! Damn! Shit, it's *already* too late for you!"

Lee blushed. He did admire the quilts, the arts and crafts, songs and dances, endearing things, and the little pot-bellied gourds that had been fashioned into hanging bird houses, he especially appreciated those. But as to how these artifacts could be as estimable as they were, and as affecting, whilst the people who accomplished it, how they could be what they certainly were... It was a mystery. But must he indeed forever go forward through life, always bidding farewell to what he had most adored? He stood, mumbled apologetically and then, because the man was drinking, went back inside the cabin. And out the other side.

His steed was waiting. Lee leapt to saddle and, because the night was green, raced downhill in exultation, because the stars were bright.

Eighteen

He woke. His spiritual condition, however, was poor. Twice, he traveled blindly from one end to the other of his three-room apartment, crossing over finally into that fourth room that had also recently become his. And so this, then, was how it was to be a gamma — a dense stupidity, like a headache that never ended. All this immediately fled away, of course, as soon as he saw the sun come thundering up in a classical display of red and purple and several kinds of gold.

On this occasion, he went directly to the lake, down along the levee and thence to shore. He knew he could not tarry there, and never mind that the strand was littered with capsized crabs, a broken harpoon, and at least four great jars half-buried in the sand with rolled-up manuscripts inside, all of it the result of last night's storm.

"It's me!" he called, but then immediately hushed when he saw that the old man was again suffering from his so-called "morning bile." Had he been vigiling here all night, this man, waiting out the storm? Certainly his hat was askew. Coming nearer, Lee marveled to see the dead leaves and other trash that had accumulated in his lap.

"Did you want to see me?" Lee asked.

"'Want?' Hardly. No, I thought it time I *should* see you. Nothing to do with 'want.'" And then: "Great Baal! Where did you get that haircut?"

Lee blushed. He had inflicted it upon himself, using for that purpose Edmund's ivory-handle knife. "Are you still feeling poorly, sir?"

"Oh, Lee, poorly indeed. It takes a lot of suffering to elicit any compassion out of *this* god. I doubt anyone has ever suffered enough for that. Look at history."

"Yes, sir." The swans were by no means beyond the man's range. Lee half-expected to see him use the cat for ammunition. Lee's other half, meanwhile, was silently urging the swans to move further away from shore.

"The word comes to me, Leland, that you think rather well of yourself."

"Sir?"

"Vaunting yourself in front of the thralls. Not good. And as if that were not enough, you've been immersing yourself — this is what they tell me — in the Hindu wisdom. Ah Lee, Lee, Lee. Someday you're going to irritate one or another of these clowns, irritate him bad, and then what will you do, hm? You don't see Philip rubbing it in people's faces, do you?"

"No, sir."

"Or is he too 'flagitious,' too?"

Lee looked down.

"No, he keeps himself under lock and key. And so should you. What? You dare to hum while I'm speaking?"

"No, sir!"

"This is *their* country, remember, and never yours. Tailored for them, not for you. Learn to keep silent, Lee, do."

"Yeah, but…!"

"Ah, Lee. You will live forever in a sphere of glass, and although they can see you, and sometimes you may see them, the best that you can expect is to communicate across the boundary with hand signals. Remember! We don't equip you here for life, Lee, but rather to supersede it."

Those were hard words, it seemed to Lee.

"Ah child, you shall see things. The Democracy grows more democratic, lower and lower, wicked and bad. Tell me, Lee, do you think you might grow up to be a tall person?"

"Maybe."

"Then beware of it when they come to lop off your head!"

Lee wrote it down, using for that purpose a narrow pad that slipped easily in and out of his vest. These days he always carried it.

"And if they ask you to serve in their wars?"

"Hide?"

"No! Great Moses, you've learned nothing at all! No, no, no; when they come for you, you must be even more enthusiastic than they!"

Lee wrote.

"And time to vote? Vote for them all!"

"'All.'"

"Serve the rich. Attend football games. Take as your model those little insects who come to resemble those whom they expect to eat."

Here Lee raised his hand: "I've read about that."

"But do you read *me*? And if you wish to get along with the poor, Lee, why, then I recommend that you begin right away issuing them commands — that's all they've ever really wanted."

"Yes, sir. I already started..."

"Would you kindly shut up while I'm speaking? Hm? And no more of this talking to yourself with accompanying lip movements. It suggests that you might be thinking. They don't like that."

Lee could hardly write fast enough.

"And smile! They *do* like that. Philip has developed a very nice one — modest, bright, quite infectious really."

That was when Lee's pencil broke.

"Or otherwise we may have to purge you, too, someday."

"Me!"

"Certainly. Or part of you, anyway. Here. And here!" He made as if he were sawing away one of Lee's arms, doing it roughly. "One more incident from you, riding nude on Mahler's Brow, and we'll toss you back into the clowns so fast that you..."

Lee, however, gazed back at him steadily. There were but six unpurged boys still remaining, and he knew for a certainty that he was at least the third-best of them, and sometimes even better than that. "Naw, you won't."

"Won't? Won't? Why, you little son-of-a-bitch!"

Lee waited for the anger; instead, after an interval, the man broke into an unwilling smile, followed by snorts and giggles and a tremendous laughter that boomed across the lake, smote Edmund's tower, and boomed right back.

"Ah, well. We may all be purged, if the money fails."

"Sir?"

"Oh, yes, I asked him — What's his name? The book fellow? — asked him to build me a working library, and do you know what he's done? He's got him the finest collection, out there in the woods, with incunabula coming out his ears, finest in the whole state of Alabama put together!"

"He's got some new ones, too."

"*That's* where it goes, *that's* why we don't have enough to eat. I might have to kill that son-of-a-bitch still!"

It was the bile. Lee opted to say nothing at first, but after a short while took up the man's fishing rod, refreshed the bait, and gave it back.

"And Lee?"

"Sir?"

"If you begin to feel that this mode of life..."

"I feel it now."

"... has simply become insupportable..."

Lee waited for the rest which, however, trailed off into snorts and sighs and popping sounds.

Nineteen

When after fresh rains, very often the woods would fill overnight with paisley flowers. Diligently he hunted and greedily he pounced each time they showed a disposition, those flowers, to make an appearance along the margins of the wold.

He liked to go off by himself and read a few pages, alone in the forest but in the presence of books. Using rose petals to mark his places, the books tended to grow bulky over time, while his brain, always pressing against the confines of its bony structure, was ruining itself on beauty, aroma, wisdom and the world. Yes, these were the first of those "episodes" — "elucidations," he called them later — that were to serve as rather different sorts of bookmarks in his long, and indeed very book-like career.

He was singing his song and smoking betimes and then ducking down behind the shrubbery every few seconds to read a few pages more. Winter had come, winter had gone, and Lee was left facing an Alabama spring, the most dangerous of all seasons. But primarily, and this was characteristic of him, he found himself probing with his free hand as he sought to garner the sun and squeeze it, and take into his own mouth some of the divine juice of which it was so full.

Such was his immodesty. The weather was so sweet, so mellow, so like what he remembered from his youth that he craved not merely to stand out in the middle of it, but rather to *participate* in it, or eat it, or better yet, *be* it. Instead, rising now and yawning and snuffing out his cigarette, he took a primrose petal and used it to mark the place to which he had advanced in the better of the two books. He had dedicated himself to reading a full twenty pages today, falling short only by a score or two. He had promised to gather mushrooms, his solemn word given to the cook. He had failed his horse as well, but had promised to atone for his neglect. Why, then, was he so plainly happy? It probably had to do with the weather.

He raced downhill, imagining the trees were enemy soldiers. Badly wounded, he leapt three creeks in consecutive succession, causing consternation in the minds of minnows and tadpoles. Lee, too, was constemed, constemed by weather which must someday, finally, drive him completely insane. Because he enjoyed a personal connection with certain of the hills? Hero of his own story—because of that? Or because, upon the advice of certain philosophers, he had turned away from "the flies of the marketplace?" Yes, all of those. Not content to be *of* it, or *in* it, or just looking at it, he hoped in time to take upon himself the duties of the weather, and hold the world within the hand that did not already hold the sun.

By early afternoon, he had come down into a clearing in the woods, where he hurriedly set about rearranging the rocks and leaves and the placement of some of the larger pine cones. At that moment, quite suddenly, Philip stepped into view. Lee perceived that he was dressed in that same jacket that bore the most arrogant inscription in the valley. He bowed, Lee did, but only very, very slightly. Philip doffed his cap.

"Rained, they say, over in Calauria County."

"Very likely."

"It might rain here."

Both men looked into the sky. There *was* a giraffe-shaped cloud, big enough and dark enough to contain some rain. But in fact, the giraffe soon loped away, abandoning four little girafflings to the immensity of the sky. Lee took one step forward, saying:

"That was a heavy assignment, Greek."

"I did mine this morning." The boy moved twenty-four inches deeper into the woods. Watching him, and thinking back upon his own last move, it seemed curious to Lee that they were drifting, not *toward* one another, but in a broad circle that skirted the shores of the clearing. Again Philip spoke up:

"I could have missed class altogether, I'd still have the best scores in school."

"Abstract concepts—Mr. Spivey thinks it's almost abnormal, the way I can, you know, deal with all that."

"Abnormal, yes. And Spivey, too."

They both took two steps. Lee thought for a moment that he could hear his horse yelling to him from far away, a warning and a caution. Nearer at hand, he saw a wren of some sort who kept glancing back and forth between the two boys, as if each boy inspired him to glance again at the one left over. Just now, the bird was glaring at Philip, his head cocked over to one side. Lee carried no weapon, of course, not unless he wished to consider his ten-ounce book as one. He took one step more. Never had he planned to say what he now heard spilling from his mouth:

"I never told anybody. And I never will — how you came up for air before I did."

"And me, I never told anybody about how you..."

But here Lee held up his hand to stop him. "Alright, OK. That makes us even, then."

"And besides, I went down before you did. And stayed longer, too."

That was only partly true. Lee took one step more. "Me," he said, "I'm always ready to die if I need to. Always."

Philip blinked. His glasses, which carried a bright blue sheen on the surface, were like a wall that cut him off from things.

"Might be better if you did," he said.

"Die?"

Philip took two steps. Hearing the bad words that had begun to pass between them, the wren lifted from his bough and flew away. Already Lee had untied the cord that held his cape. He needed only to hoist it up into full view, filling the other boy's vista with the words embossed on it in blood-red lettering.

"*Vivrai toujours*," said Lee, reading it aloud in proper accent. For indeed, it was precisely this slogan of his that enabled him to remain "always ready to die." He took two steps more, halting when he saw that Philip was in the process of getting out of his jacket, and very soon now would be in further process — Lee dreaded it — of showing what had been knitted on it by grace of Arnsdorf's wife.

"I know what it says!"

Too late. The boy, brilliant boy, now raised high the jacket with one hand. And now Lee must once more gaze upon it, the word "PRIMUS" emblazoned in gold, and just beneath it the arrogant picture of a block of glass, or prism rather, splitting a ray of light into the six constituent colors — red, yellow, purple, and several others — representing the institution's primary disciplines of philosophy, music, German, botany, and Greek. Shaken by it, Lee gave ground. Seven seconds went by slowly as he stood transfixed by the word and symbol.

"I see it."

"Yes! *Toujours*, that's how long you'll see it."

Lee could feel a headache coming on, a thudding development originating at the juncture of the cortex and spine. He was close to rushing upon the boy, of beating him into non-existence, of calling for his well-hoofed horse or Edmund's knife. But in truth, his headache had grown too serious to let him do anything except…

Take another step. Meanwhile, the other boy had gotten back into his jacket, had taken out his book, and was calmly scanning up and down the page. Lee now fully expected to see him pluck out one of his perfectly-sharp pencils and begin making a little drawing in the margin of the text. Somehow they had circled around one another in such a way that both men were standing in about the same position from which they had started out. Such was Lee's headache that he thought it inadvisable to rush upon the boy at this time.

"Rained, they say." He doffed his cap.

"Yes. Calauria County." The other boy bowed, though only very slightly.

Twenty

Month by month his powers improved. He was getting heartily sick of it, too.

One night, while stretched out at full length on the carpet, Lee suddenly rolled over and lay face-up. Arnsdorf, he saw, had lapsed off to sleep in front of his floor-to-ceiling bookcase. Still, he stood in no danger of any kind, not with his wife standing guard at his side. Lee crawled nearer, striving to get a more detailed view of the man's plump, baby-like, pouting face where, between the dewlap and the lips, one of the world's greater green warts was getting larger by the day. His gown — he wore it everywhere — was green also, and was adorned with a silk rose and velvet thorn, said to have come down to him "from Wagner."

"Yes," said his woman, "he's old now. And yet at one time, he thought that he had been appointed to change the whole direction of modern education."

"The *whole* direction?"

"Why, yes. *Away* from utility. *Towards* aesthetics. Yes, he was naïve. And someday, Lee, you'll be naïve, too."

Lee doubted it.

"Yes, naïve. Imagine! Trusting to his 'God of Beauty' to bring it all about."

Lee, the better to reflect upon what he had heard, drew back a few inches.

"But I'm sure you'll see to it, Leland, that our god does score one, small victory someday. Just one? Will you see to that?"

"One, yes, ma'am. Shall we put on *Tristan* now?"

"No, we're listening to something else just at this moment."

"Yes, ma'am. Mozart."

That was when Lee recognized that the man had come awake and was spying down at him narrowly between his toad-like lids. Even now, after all his work and efforts, Lee had not passed *all* the qualitative tests this man expected from students of his.

"You can just leave that machine alone, thank you."

"Yes, sir."

"It's mine and I own it."

"I know."

"You have your own machine."

"Yes, sir; you gave it to me. And I can remember my surprise."

"I did. In order that you might leave mine alone. Oh, Leland, Leland, what is it, really, that you hate so much about my favorite" — the Eighteenth — "century?" He now appeared to fall to sleep again. Even so, Lee could still detect some little part of the actual eye, green and evil, that glinted from beneath the inch-thick lid. "Leland, Leland, oh. And are you quite comfortable, lying there on your belly in my fluffy warm rug?"

Lee thought about it. "Yes, sir."

"And the meal — was it sufficient to the need? The sweet potatoes?"

"With marshmallows on top? Yes, sir."

"Good, good. Good." Again, he seemed to sleep. "I don't know about you, Leland, I just don't. Of all the boys still hanging on here, I would say that you alone have the smallest appreciation of my favorite century."

"But I'm real good at abstract concepts. Dr. Spivey now, he claims that I…"

"Spare me."

"And French. Boy howdy, I'm *really* good at that."

"Philip — *that's* where the talent is. He likes my century."

But at this, Lee held up his hand to stop him. "Naw, that won't work anymore — trying to get us to do better than each other all the time."

"Indeed! *He* saw through it two months ago."

"Two!"

"Thought you said it didn't work anymore."

Lee glared. His cloak was in the vestibule. "Well, I reckon I'll take my leave now." He stood. "But I want to thank you for the wine and all the other fixings."

"And for the machine I gave you? Sit, boy, sit. All right, we'll play something else. Lord, Lord, Lord. Dear, will you bring the boy his favorite opera? She's going. Look at that, she used to be so young, my wife, so lovely. It's all my fault; I'll burn for this. You want her to do some sewing while you're here? And Lee, really you ought to have a bath once in a while."

"Can't."

"'Can't?'"

"Lake's too muddy."

"Oh, Lord."

They drank more wine, followed shortly after by some of the woman's ten o'clock biscuits, wonderful ones filled to overflowing with authentic butter. Lee was grateful alike for their warmth as for the bright green jelly made from quinces to which both men were hopelessly addicted.

"What is *Time*, Lee, so-called, and whence does it come?"

"Well, I reckon…"

"And Light! What is *that*? Time and Light, Light and Motion. But Lee! What is Beauty — that's what *we* need to know."

"Well…" The jelly was good, but did that mean that the man had to consume it by the quart?

"Now these forebears of yours, Lee, decent-enough people I suppose, what knew *they* of Beauty, hm? Nothing."

"My grandfather, he…"

"To be sure. But I'm talking *real* Beauty, Lee, big stuff — whence comes *that*? Why, Lord, it could mean the end of someone like you, Beauty like that. Too small, too naïve already, you wouldn't be able to stand up to it."

Long ago and far away, Lee could feel his gorge begin to rise.

"Extinction, Lee, that's what gives beauty to things. See that patch of bare earth over there?" He pointed, in fact, to the carpet.

"Yes, sir."

"Good! And did you know that at one time, a loving couple stood just there, he loving her and her him almost more than they could bear?"

"I didn't, no, sir."

"No? Well, perhaps it was over there, that patch over yonder by the lamp stand. They must have assumed that their little affair would pass away into oblivion, with no one left to remember it. They didn't know about you and me."

For a long time, Lee stood staring at the patch.

"You can survive, Lee, without Beauty, but what you cannot do is live. And even here among us now, a majority of the boys shall taste it never. Ah, well, and perhaps that's best. Let even a child but taste it once… Certainly *I* wouldn't want to be responsible for something like that."

There was a long, mournful, and very depressing silence. He had a pretty good idea, Lee did, of the question coming up next.

"Lee?"

"Sir?"

"Have *you* been tasting it?"

Lee lowered his eyes. The opera was approaching that part where he would need all his resources to keep from breaking down in front of these people.

"Lee?"

But Lee was not taking any more questions.

His cloak was where he had left it, but he had been wrong about the condition of the lake. It was while he was moving toward it, humming and thinking, his head full of bees, that Lee turned fourteen.

Twenty-one

They gathered in the village, Arnsdorf, Lee, all of them except for the Director himself, who was absent in Atlanta on a matter of taxes, it was said.

Today the tavern was closed, which is to say until Arnsdorf began pounding with great force upon the massy door. The hosteller was in sleeping clothes, the tassel of his night cap dangling down in front of his eye.

"Professor! I thought it might be you. The noise. Enter, enter please; we're flattered you could come."

They were escorted with courtesy to the far table where a storm lantern hung from the rafter. Right away, Arnsdorf demanded a black beer for himself, wine for the bibliographer and sweet tea for the boys. As impatient as he conspicuously was, nevertheless he allowed Spivey to begin the discussion.

"Came winter, bringing chills…"

"Get on with it!"

"Winter. Am I also to be held accountable for that? Winter and other things following hard upon? 'Abandon then ye all hope…'" and so on.

Lee poured the tea. It would need another fifteen minutes before the man finally got down to the substance of his quarrel with Goldman. Still whining, the book steward now drew from his pouch a remarkable-looking volume bound in hide and branded in gold. They could not but marvel at it, all nine men.

"My fault, then? Prices being what they are? Explain it to me, Young Edmund, if you can—how to put together a usable assemblage of books without paying prices for them. And fie upon prices, anyhow!"

"See how he gives away our substance to book dealers?" Arnsdorf said. "Blackguards, most of them."

Young Burchem raised his hand and waited to be acknowledged. "What book is it?"

"You ask. Very well, I am here to report that I have taken possession of the third-best—and that should particularly resonate with you, Leland, third-best—the third-best surviving copy of Cockayne's *Leechdoms*. Just look at it!"

They stroked it, touching it in various places, Arnsdorf included. Now, taking the thing back into his own clutches, the librarian began slowly and obscenely turning through the innumerable illustrations, exceptionally fine ones rendered by a hand that had wanted to give full credence to the author and the prose.

"Hand-colored plates gentlemen, yes, and high-grade workmanship, too, as you will agree. Just look!"

"How much?"

"Dear old Cockayne! He was the first of those who finally came to admit that certain natural things, leaves and seeds, how they bear likeness to those same glands in whose weal they..."

"How much did it cost?"

"In whose weal. More wine please."

"And how much, if I may ask again, did you pay for the goddamn thing!"

"The price will appreciate, I absolutely guarantee it. And so never mind how much soever I might have paid for it! Let that remain between Goldman, and between me." And then: "But why have we gathered here, gentlemen?"

Lee filled his glass, filling it this time with wine. Was he the only one to have seen that the town cobbler, a low fellow, leathery in complexion, and the glazier, a person of transparently bad character, had settled in the next alcove and were smoking silently as they listened to the professors and the alphas? Arnsdorf, in the meantime, his patience completely at an end, was unfurling a large-scale map and, using beer bottles and books to hold it flat, was pointing at it in the meager light with his frankfurter-sized index finger.

"Mexico," he quoth, tapping at it.

"Sir?"

"Because of the price of things in Mexico—that's why I chose it."

They all looked around at one another. Mexico was brown, according to the map, and contained any number of whimsically-shaped provinces. Said Arnsdorf:

"No one knows the truth about taxes, and not even the Director himself knows for certain which of those bonds may still be valid.

Most likely we'll remain right..." He touched it. "... right here in our beautiful valley!"

"Shall we make the move together in one group?" Philip asked.

"No. In twos and threes, I should think. After all, we don't want to alert the..." He glanced at the cobbler, who had gone away. Lee could not entirely determine whether the glazier was still there. Accordingly, they all now drew more closely around the music professor, who was tracing out the two alternate routes that connected north-northeastern Alabama to an almost perfectly analogous locale inside Mexico. It looked to Lee like a great many square miles of nothing, and the promise of a very fundamental sort of life available in a place such as that. He glanced at Philip, finding that the boy had already begun to sketch an array of three different varieties of cactus plants in the borders of the map. This was what puzzled Lee, that the boy could be what he was, his glasses peerless and his hair close-trimmed, while his own personal satchel remained as untidy as it did, with things hanging out.

It was mid-morning, the glazier having left and come back again before Lee climbed down from the bench and went around to Spivey.

"I don't think you paid too much," he said.

"Far too much. Couldn't help myself."

"I know."

"Young Edmund gets no wine?"

"Shoot, no," said Lee. "Edmund's still thirteen."

Hurriedly, they finished off their drinks. They faced a twenty-minute stroll back to the institution, not to mention those who liked to read along the way.

Twenty-two

The *bibliomane* continued in distant parts, a jumbled cottage, never fully painted, on the further side of town. Of the clowns and churls, *they*, at least, had the sense to keep a fire in weather like this. Not so Lee's friend, who today was standing out in someone else's yard, his smile fixed upon what admittedly was a preternatural sky, *too* blue really, and dangerous to gaze upon. Lee therefore turned his own, somewhat smaller attention to the spumes of smoke emerging from the chimneys, a feline stuff that lifted and dawdled and smelled predominantly of rosin. Now, broaching near, he yanked three times at the man's pajama shirt.

"Ah, yes! Young Pefley, is it?"

"I came."

"I see! And after all the hard things I said about you, too! No, I'll suffer for that. But tell me quick—do you come bringing any little gifts, perchance? Items of soap, for example? Or examples of other things? I can't hear you."

"No funds," Lee said, blushing.

"No, of course not. I could have loaned you the funds, however, as well you know."

Thus they stood, each man slightly embarrassed by the other and by the alarmed-looking old woman on the porch trying to shoo them away.

"Ah, Lee," the man said. "Lovely here, is it not? But as for that rustic down yonder riding in his buggy, why, he appears to have stepped forth from out of a tableau by Bruegel himself, no? Come, I'll show you!"

They raced to the cottage, which proved dark, full of mildew, and stinking of binder's glue. Lee was only in small part surprised to find the room full of packing equipment, rolls of tape, and buckets of confetti. So far as he was able to judge, the man had succeeded in wrapping just one single package of books, an untidy effort that gave Lee the beginnings of a headache.

"Oh, Lee, I do so hope old Goldman can cash those bonds. Otherwise it's back to Yale for me. See here?"

It was a massive book, or portfolio rather, holding pictures of some very brutish-looking peasants who did in truth bear a close resemblance to the farmers in the valley.

"And yet they get so mad when I show it to them!"

"Nothing surprises me, not anymore."

"Nor will they come visit anymore. Lee, Lee, it's a skewed-up world that considers *us* to be skewed, Lee, you and me."

"Yes, sir. The Greeks now, they used to…"

"Take my advice — either seek power absolute, or else have nothing to do with people."

He jotted it down. "The Greeks, they…"

"There are only two sorts of worlds ,Lee, both quite bad."

"Two."

"Why, yes. The world of buying and selling, or the life of war. Turn your back on both, Lee, that's my behest to thee."

"In other words, I could just turn my back on both of 'em."

"What! And spend the whole of your career in bitter isolation? You're hard, Lee, hard and cold. How came you to be so very hard and cold? Was it those juvenile detentions of '46 and '49? So dreadful, were they?"

"Which did Philip choose?"

"Hm?"

"Power absolute? Or nothing to do with folks?"

"And now, I think, is time for the wine."

They debated for hours, Lee doing most of the actual packaging. But when it came to those hundred-pound volumes with gold dust on the fore edges of which Yale had formerly been so proud, Lee found that he could place but one such book in each individual carton. And even then, there was very little space left over for the confetti. Meanwhile, the librarian had gotten drunk, leaving Lee to do the work without so much as a second cup of wine. Lee could hear him from time to time, mumbling in the background.

"Ten thousand souls — surely that's not too few for a globe as reduced as this one."

Lee nodded, adding, "And then everybody could have his own square mile."

"Some in pasture and some in woods. Yes, and some in fallow, too."

Together they thought about it, woods and fallow. Urged on by the songs of horned cattle, the afternoon was changing over into night.

"Ah, Lee, if only the bonds prove good." And then, a minute having gone past in the increasing dim: "Lee! Are you still here?"

The boy raised his hand.

"Ah, yes. Speak, Lee, and do it quickly. Night is coming on."

"Each man his thousand acres..."

"Yes?"

"... therefore each man his thousand books."

"Ha!" It seemed to satisfy him. Radiant in the face, he corked the wine (it was empty), an action that stood as his own personal pledge to drink no further from that particular vessel. Lee went on:

"And each man his wife, too."

"'Wives,' you say. But what manner of wife Lee? It does matter, you realize. No, you'll just have to trust me about that."

"Nineteenth-century wives."

"Nineteen! You're shrewd, Lee. A goodly wife for thee! So let *her* be your reward — goodly, cheerful, and loyal."

"Bosomy, too."

"Lee! You horrify me. Oh, all right, that, too. A devil in bed let her be, and a goodly cook for thee. All this I grant in return for your excellent method of packaging books."

But Lee's mind was galloping far out in advance. Or rather, galloping far into the past. "A Greek wife."

"And why not? Certainly the menfolk had little enough use for them."

"Penelope."

"Careful, Leland; that's Mycenaean stuff you're talking about now."

"Andromache, she..."

"Two wives! Nay, Lee, let us return to the books, shall we? For we have very little time left to us, if you're to describe all thousand of them."

"Yes, sir. These books, they..."

"Incunabula — I read only these. Some on vellum, some not, some with gold rust all around the edges — it's evil of you, Lee, to mention those."

Lee looked down.

"And what sort of weather is it, Lee? *Reading* weather, I mean."

"Clouds will be six miles thick. Nighttime all day long."

"That would make it tenebrous indeed. But domicile, Lee, tell about that."

"The domicile. It's several stories high, Mr. Spivey, and has a turret with a blue tile roof. I've seen pictures of it."

"This turret…"

"For the books. But it could also hold a wife."

"You haven't said a word about the outside landscape, Lee."

"Swamps, sir, all swamps and fen."

"Proceed. You're doing well."

"Mountains in the distance with fog and smoke coming off the summits. And volcanoes, sir; they go on burning for thousands of years and when finally extinct, they end up holding purified lakes in 'the palms of their hands,' so to speak."

"No, Lee, stop. It's simply not credible, a fourteen-year-old making utterances like these. Just stop."

"And then one day to come to a high place, thence to spy down upon the remains of a town — and you know which one — a town all ruint and burnt," and so on.

"Stop."

"Ah, Spivey, Spivey." He stood. The man was wearing a placid expression such that Lee believed that he could predict for him a fine sleep persisting for hours among the litter. Accordingly, he now tiptoed from the cottage, sneaked down the lane, leapt the creek, and went quickly over the hill. Until he heard a faint voice, hoarse and distant:

"Careful, boy! The dangers."

His job now was to bypass town, if he could, and then take a direct path through the awful woods. He would not be pestered by clowns, not if he avoided all exposure to them. On this occasion, he saw no widows sentineling on their porches, nor hounds, nor moths congregated about the street lamps. The moon was down. It was owing solely to his extreme acuity, made more extreme by danger, that he was able to pick out the trail, itself made more than ordinarily vague by the six-mile clouds that sent him off in the wrong direction and harassed him as he fled.

Twenty-three

In the days that followed he had two letters, dark ones, from Adalgisa. He read both carefully, finally sharing one of them, the least disturbing of the two, with Arnsdorf. Rumors of rumors, rumors of wrath, rumors that the people no longer believed it was a Bible School. And then at night, he would very often light the lamp, take the letters and spread them on the table. He had his suspicions, based upon the two distinct colors of ink that the girl had felt "compelled" to use, that these sheets probably incorporated a secret message code, if only he could break it. Thus Lee believed. Confronted with scads of botany and loads of Greek, nevertheless he continued to waste his time with Adalgisa.

He should have known from the beginning that all things must finally come to an end. Especially, he should have known it when, after a three-hour sojourn in the library, he would emerge to find a number of Alabama State Highway Patrolmen scanning the valley with binoculars. A week of this and he began to recognize some of the individuals, including a certain red-faced personality who operated a high-powered telescope from the warmth of his car. These instruments, and the uncultivated types who used them, could they, from that distance, decipher the titles that Lee carried under his arm? Quickly, he made an adjustment by turning the books to face each other, condemning the patrolmen to go through eternity with unanswered questions. He hated to pass beneath the gaze of these people, and always tried to wear a calm and guilt-free expression whenever it was necessary to do so.

For it had come to this, that Goldman, taking a half-gross of books along with him, had decamped for Mexico ten days ago. Not that he could transfer Spivey's whole collection in that way — far from it! No, these days when Lee went to visit, very often he saw door-size crates exiting town in the bay of horse-drawn wagons, or carried on trucks, or, in one instance, moving southward on an apparatus mounted on bicycle wheels. And Spivey himself? He was over-worked at this time, nervous to a degree, and lived on wine.

Apart from that, all things went forward as in the past. Greek never ended, and never would Lee get clear of some of those conjugations that kept him awake until three at night. Good at substantives, poor with enclitics, awful in the management of particles, lately he had been giving his attention mostly to aorist participles. French, however, *had* ended, its place taken over by three and four hours every day of accelerated study in the Italian tongue. Botany also went forward, and appropriately so, now that it was spring.

And because it was spring, Lee felt a renewed interest in his horse, driving him each day further and further into the wold.

"You'll have to cut him free." (Arnsdorf.)

"What!"

"Free. Unless you want him on a diet of mesquite."

Others things continued forward, too. He still dove to the bottom of the lake from time to time, remaining there for 200 seconds or more, or until his head began to rot. Or go two days without food — these were just some of his methods for showing contempt for normal people and the outside world. He wrote to 'Gisa, mostly in code, devoting the greater part of the letter to pure trivia, just as she had always done. Philip had left three days ago, giving Lee an additional five rooms in which he now had more space than books. Edmund, too, went forward, turning fourteen on the exact same day that he came to Lee, shook with him, uttered a joke or two, and then began to speak feelingly about the dangers they had surmounted together, and the even more threatening dangers they could expect in passing through Texas. Again, they shook.

"Goldman's chair..."

"Yes! Sinking into the sand."

"Philip left three days ago."

"Hmm. He'll be in Mississippi by now."

"Moving fast."

They laughed.

"Your horse, I reckon you'll have to..."

But here Lee held up his hand to stop him. His cigarettes were gone, finished, and although he continued to carry the empty package about for nostalgia's sake, he had nothing to offer his friend.

"Arnsdorf's going to burn the buildings down, all of 'em."

"What!"

"Doesn't want the clowns to inherit them — that's what he said."

"Oh, well. Nothing surprises me, not anymore."

"Me, neither, I'm just as unsurprised as you are."

They shook.

"You won't be wearing your cloak, will you, while you're in Texas?"

Lee stopped him. "When do *you* leave?"

"Wednesday. But I turned fourteen this morning."

They shook.

Years now passed, or rather a few days in which the number of pages he read were those of most peoples' years. Again he jumped into the Hindu wisdom and again came out unscathed. Finally, on the twenty-seventh of that month, he borrowed Arnsdorf's key, a heavy item of about fourteen inches in length, and carried it in both arms across the levee.

A strange silence pervaded the stable, a condition that explained itself when at last he pulled open the door and found some half-dozen gammas lying about at random in the darkness. As heavily medicated as they were, Lee feared no trouble from them. He therefore concentrated upon the hens and, after chasing them down one by one and lifting them out through the window, encouraged them, for the first time in their lives, to make a proper use of their wings. Useless — they simply ran around to the open door and filed back inside again. The hogs, the hogs were suspicious, which is to say until he had prodded the king of them out into the night, across the field and over the hill. Amid all that noise and grunting, not one thrall opened so much as just one of his eyes. Intrigued by their behavior, Lee approached with the lantern, but then at once jumped back in high alarm when he saw the devolution that had taken place in their features and the wheezing sounds they gave off. He knew this much about them, that they had more life to be burnt, gutted, and minced than to read a good book, a moral principle, as he later learned, that obtained as well for the general public.

The mules, on the other hand, or other hoof rather, had deserved well of the community, and it gave Lee some considerable pleasure to usher them to freedom at last. Dignified to the end, they departed one by one, pausing only to remark upon the unwonted brightness of the moon. Clouds, too — they fled past overhead in high numbers, pushed by the currents of spring. Lee next made haste to the cows, who might also be drugged, judging by their passivity.

"Ah, me," Lee said to himself, "many a time we have relied upon your gifts of milk, yes, and butter, too, not even to mention cheese." He did not actually utter such things out loud, not unless he had wanted to confuse the creatures with English words. Meanwhile, the hens had come back again and were roosting on their former perches.

The horses were next. To steel himself, Lee hummed and twiddled, trying to think about other things. Figments of world literature sped through his brain, trailed closely by irregular declensions. The mare was tawny, her bright eyes full of experience and old, long-ago forgotten episodes. Lee whispered good things into her ear and then opened the stall and hied her on her way. Very little sugar remained to him; nevertheless, he now took out his last five cubes and distributed them among the gelding and the goat. His own horse got nothing, not yet. For such an animal as that, Lee had special words, other gifts, and cautions to impart. He had never in his life been guilty of crying, not since he had turned fourteen, and had no intention whatsoever of being observed in that activity. Accordingly, he did nothing more for several minutes while waiting quietly for the chapter to come to its end.

Twenty-four

His time running out, Lee frequented the village more and more, laboring every day to barter some of his less necessary things for supplies and cigarettes. His Hindu books went to the grocer, Lee coming away with two bushels of Georgia peaches.

Or, he might run up to the top of the tower and dangle there for a minute or two for old time's sake. Or — and he did this but one time only — he might toss a few pebbles up against what he believed to be Adalgisa's second-story window, getting nothing in return but an old man, largely bald. Or, he would stand perfectly still at the edge of the highway and then run out from under the draymen's sputum at the last moment. Or, very frequently, go and loiter hungrily at the baker's shop until a woman chanced along. These were his tendencies and this his village, right up until the day there came to town two odd-looking individuals representing The Yale University Library's Rare Books Division.

"Odd-looking," he said, although they might have passed for normal in the North. Lee, still loitering, cast his glance heavenward and began humming his special song. He carried a slingshot for cosmetic reasons, that he might be considered an authentic boy, and had the county's most adored dog snoozing next to him on the sidewalk. He liked to imagine that he was more or less indistinguishable from the general population; instead, the odder of the two men immediately pointed him out and came forward.

The other man was just as odd. He had parts and pieces of a beard and carried a briefcase so thin and polished, with silver clasps, it could not have weighed much more than the list of books, very neatly typed, that it undoubtedly contained. Once before, Lee had found himself confronted by a person of this sort, at the time of his original kidnapping.

"That's a very… *handsome* dog you've got there."

Lee looked at the dog. "Naw. Too flagitious." These were men, not women; nevertheless, Lee now turned and gazed sorrowfully toward the cinnamon rolls.

"And what — you don't mind if we ask? — what two books are those you carry there, face-to-face beneath your arm?"

Lee looked for his arm, looking first at the wrong one. He knew, of course, that the titles were inscribed legibly on the spines and could easily be identified by any who could read Greek.

"You go to that... *school*, don't you?"

Lee jumped back. "I used to, yes, sir. Once. But now it's all gone."

"*Je doute de ta parole.*"

"*Hélas! C'est vrai tout même.*"

Both men jumped back. Across the way, the tinker had come to his door and was regarding the conversation darkly. Would he, or would he not, fly to Lee's aid in case of need? Certainly he had the tools for it. That was when the more truly odd of the two men, the one with the goatee, got down on one knee, making himself even shorter than Lee. Lee was prepared to talk to him either in French, Italian, or Greek; instead it was plain, northern speech that he now heard.

"Stancil Spivey — you know him?"

"Sir?"

"Tall man, glassine teeth. Take us there and you'll have all the cinnamon rolls you can carry in your other hand."

Lee looked to the rolls. There were other things in that window that he prized even more highly than those.

"Who?"

"Stancil Spivey."

"Real tall person, funny teeth?"

"Why, yes."

"Got lots of books?"

"Yes! Exactly!"

Lee smiled. Using his free hand, he had pulled out his left-side pocket and had let the lining hang down, his way of showing how empty it was. He had to react when he saw how quickly they replied, both men suddenly thrusting on him two large bills of currency with the portraits of certain psychotic northern generals on them. He counted the money twice, and after folding each bill in his fastidious way, hid some of it in his vest, some his pants, some in the books, and some in the lining of his hat. He knew this, that if he took off running just now, Yale had not men enough — they never had — to drag him back. Instead, he coughed once, politely, and then pointed out the location of the grocer and his Hindu books.

All afternoon until the sun was gone — that was the amount of time that Lee spent in his rooms, alone. He had been roaming at will up and down the dormitory, visiting and revisiting his possessions, labeling some of them, reorganizing others, and checking now and again beneath the cot. Two times he heard his horse, now clearly in trouble, calling hoarsely from far-off locations. He smoked and hummed and then placed himself at his second-best desk and scribbled off a quick letter to the girl which, however, dissatisfied him, and which he then threw away. He had books on all sides, all of them clamoring to be taken to Mexico. He also had assignments pending, and at least fifteen verbs of hideous complexity that needed to be memorized before next Thursday; instead, he had given the past half-hour to wading barefooted up and down, around the corner and into other rooms as he sought for lost pennies in the carpet nap.

He was sure that night had come and was surprised to find that the sun had simply run down into a niche between the hills. To look more closely at it, he stepped outside, climbed the levee, and was directing himself toward the lake when he came to a complete and sudden stop owing to…

The geology professor. Arnsdorf, too, was there, his wife as well, not to mention a certain pale alpha, originally from Jasper, whose extreme taciturnity had at one time caused him to be regarded as "the best of them all." Exhausted from his run, Lee strove to put on a bored expression. It distressed him that a man like that, as old as he was and as easily distracted as Lee knew him to be, should have elected to make the journey on foot with a knapsack on his back, a staff in one hand, and a broad-brim hat to ward off the sun.

They all went down to the boundary together, the masters lining up in order of rank to shake the man's hand and say farewell. Last came Lee, whose own hand was somewhat etiolated from lack of exercise and too much reading.

"How now, Pefley?" the paleontologist said. "Soon we shall be gathering our fossils, you and I, albeit in a more southerly clime!"

Lee, who seriously doubted it, proceeded to laugh with great merriment — until he saw that he was laughing alone.

"Shoot, yeah!" he said. "You'll get there, no doubt about it. And then we'll..."

"Fossils."

"Yeah!'

Mrs. Arnsdrof, weeping, now stepped forth and handed over to the man a decorated basket with hot biscuits and a bottle of bright green jelly hidden in the bunting.

"Now, Warren..."

"I'll be careful."

"It's your age, Warren."

"Yes, but who would wish to steal *that*?"

They all broke out laughing with a jollity that came to an end before Lee could arrange to participate in it. He had arrived without any sort of gift for the man, not even so much as a handkerchief with which to wave him on his way. Seeing how the man hobbled and limped, and to guess at the heaviness of his knapsack, Lee had but small faith in his chances.

He ran back home in the dark. The moon was up, sun down, fog rising, and him with more pages than he liked to think about before it was time to sleep, sleep and rise, rise and read and... That was when he smote himself on the forehead. Amid so much tumultuousness, he had forgotten to choose his themes for tonight's onrushing dreams!

Twenty-five

The time was nigh. But when Tuesday came, and he still had thirty pages of Thucydides in front of him, and when this was followed by still other days, the work growing harder, at that time Lee went up into the hills, but then soon came down again when he saw that he had misjudged the weather.

Dark did come, arriving just moments before Lee had finished the last of the pages, had snapped the book shut, and had forced the unused ink from his pen, returning it to the bottle wherein the multifarious colors — and nothing ever surprised him anymore — refused to blend. Greek was done, or for the nonce at any rate, and geology too, and other fields as well. Never had he felt so strange.

Four times he sampled the night, each time running back to his room after but a short delay. Finally, with the blackness-and-stars coefficient having reached the pitch that he demanded in stars that belonged to him, he remained indoors no longer. Anyone watching from a distance would have had to be satisfied with only the most fleeting glimpse — cape flying, arms outstretched — as he raced directly into the hills.

Arrogance clove to him and exhilaration drove his blood. Far below him, he saw the lake where, deep within, the eternal furnace of the night was pulsing still, feeding on fuel fetched by gars. Climbing higher, he crashed into a realm of smoke and fog and came out sputtering. These conifers and larches, they welcomed him graciously. Lee recognized in them the souls of Grecians who had died nobly during the Fable Age. Were it not for that, no one could know where he was just now, not even those one or two who might still remember his name. And meanwhile, all the time that someone might hypothetically be watching from afar through binoculars or a telescope, Lee's name was not likely known, even to him.

Dark was the valley, save only where Goldman had run off and left his bulb glowing. Scanning further and shielding his eyes, Lee perceived the city of Birmingham now once again stewing in its own late-night juices. Would he, Leland, prove to be that city's destroyer? The one to plow it with salt and scatter its remnants far? Almost certainly not — it was simply too early in the ongoing unfolding of Alabama's history. Would another do it for him someday? Oh, yes. But when he bethought him then of the number of such cities, their names and other qualities, their narrow lanes and all the girls they contained, fourteen-year-olds with arms outstretched, all of them in danger of bestowing their love upon lesser men than he... And when he pondered the adventures that lay in wait for him, accusing himself at the same time of having transgressed through too much reading... And when he admitted how, hereafter, all things must seem very trivial that were not very great... And especially when compared to music... And how that for him there were to be no friends, and never another valley like this one, no country of his own... And when he thought... And when he considered... Well! It went to his head like wine.

By just past midnight, he had broken though the weald, had jumped two creeks, and stood, listing grievously from too much beauty too quickly brought before him, tottering on the wold. Between him and the stars, he had been carrying on so outrageously, pushing his luck, so that he had actually come to believe that there was nothing he could not eventually accomplish. And yet, anyone watching for him, such a person like that would have lost sight of him altogether in a field as dark as this one, the boy himself so small, the world so broad, and night what it was, too. That person, what really could he know about the matters that contended inside Leland's head? The beauties, for example, that filled his rods and cones and had him on his knees begging for an end to it? That person, would he see that it was only Lee again, Lee at night, dazzled quite, asking still? No. For although Lee was there, that "person" wasn't.

Other books published by Arktos:

Beyond Human Rights
by Alain de Benoist

The Problem of Democracy
by Alain de Benoist

Germany's Third Empire
by Arthur Moeller van den Bruck

The Arctic Home in the Vedas
by Bal Gangadhar Tilak

Revolution from Above
by Kerry Bolton

Metaphysics of War
by Julius Evola

The Path of Cinnabar: An Intellectual Autobiography
by Julius Evola

Archeofuturism
by Guillaume Faye

Why We Fight
by Guillaume Faye

The WASP Question
by Andrew Fraser

The Saga of the Aryan Race
by Porus Homi Havewala

The Owls of Afrasiab
by Lars Holger Holm

De Naturae Natura
by Alexander Jacob

Fighting for the Essence
by Pierre Krebs

Can Life Prevail?
by Pentti Linkola

A Handbook of Traditional Living
by Raido

The Jedi in the Lotus: Star Wars and the Hindu Tradition
by Steven J. Rosen

It Cannot Be Stormed
by Ernst von Salomon

Tradition & Revolution
by Troy Southgate

Against Democracy and Equality: The European New Right
by Tomislav Sunic

The Initiate: Journal of Traditional Studies
by David J. Wingfield (ed.)

Lightning Source UK Ltd.
Milton Keynes UK
UKOW040609210413

209519UK00001B/8/P